A Daddy for Christmas 2: Foster

GABBI GREY

F oster

I'm a successful entrepreneur who's made a good life for himself. I've had a few intimate relationships, but none have lasted. Probably because I haven't been able to be my authentic self. See, in my heart, I'm a pup. I want to curl into a wonderful Daddy's lap and be petted, stroked, and praised. I long for piles with other puppies where we play and I can make friends. But who's going to accept a forty-five-year-old man into that puppy pile?

Arnav

I met Foster on Halloween, and I wanted him because he was good-looking and hot, despite being twenty years my senior. Now, when I spot him across a BDSM playroom, I'm struck by his forlorn look. I haven't seen him here on puppy-play night before, but I'm not surprised when he tells me he wants to be a pup. I was born to be a Daddy. For Foster, I'm ready to dive into the world of sweet pups and handlers and see if I have what it takes to make Foster's Christmas wish come true.

Foster is an age-gap interracial gay romance about a lonely pup, a younger Daddy, and the best Christmas imaginable.

A Daddy for Christmas 2 is a multi-author series. Holiday tales of lost boys in need of Daddy's love and in some cases, a firm hand. Naughty or nice, it's all in Santa's hands now. So why not dive in and read each standalone and enjoy the holidays alongside our boys.

multimedia, audio, or other medium. We support the right of humans to control their artistic works.

No generative AI was used in the creation of this book.

Edits by ELF

Cover by Jo Clement

Dedication

Reshma

Kaje

Renae

ELF

Wendy

T.L. and the other authors

Contents

Prologue

Foster

I first saw the man of my dreams at Quinton's infamous Halloween party. The man I set eyes on was tall, lithe, with tanned skin, and a shy smile that made my heart flutter...and my cock sit up and take notice.

That smile he offered to a young lady in a Superwoman costume. Wait, no, Wonder Woman. And man, did she ever pull off the look. I might not be into ladies, but I could appreciate a gorgeous one when I spotted her.

Sexy man looked up and caught my gaze.

I fought my instinct to immediately look away. I didn't *know* he was gay. If gaydar existed, I certainly hadn't been gifted with it. God found me easy to play with. Showing me someone who might be interesting—might be worth taking a second look at—and then they turned out to be straight.

Or worse, queer, but not interested in a washed-up, forty-something, gay man who could barely articulate he was a homosexual. Most men just didn't have time for my shit.

Hell, I didn't have time for my shit.

Handsome man leaned in to whisper something into Wonder Woman's ear.

She grinned, cut a glance my way, then turned her attention back to him. She pressed a hand to his arm, offered a beatific smile, and gestured to me with her chin.

He smiled broadly and then headed my way.

Only when he was within a few feet did I take in his colorful costume. I cocked my head as he stopped before me—right in my personal space. "Octopus?" Somehow, I got the word out.

The eight purple ropes painted like tentacles likely should've been a clue, but sometimes I could be a little slow on the uptake. I didn't have a lot of experience with costumes. Or parties. Especially costume parties.

He bestowed that devastating grin on me. "Yes. Kind of pathetic."

Boldly, I fingered a tentacle. "I think it's...creative."

He laughed. "Well, it's something. I shouldn't offer excuses, but work's kicking my ass these days."

I offered a smile. "What do you do?"

"You'll laugh."

I appeared to consider tapping my chin. "Octopus wrangler? You'd need a lot of experience with tentacles."

He burst out laughing. "Lawyer, but I'm going to have to remember that one. Octopus wrangler. Not much need for them in Mission City, I wouldn't think."

"No clue. I work in construction." Better to get that on the table quickly. I'd met with at least two guys who'd been so snobby that they'd politely made excuses and abandoned me in the middle of dates like I was covered in mud. I was a foreman, for Christ's sake. I helped out on the job site, but mostly I supervised. And I sure as fuck showered after each workday.

Gorgeous guy's dark-brown eyes lit. "Okay, not something I know much about. But you can enlighten me, right? I love learning about other people. Unless you don't want to talk shop, which I totally respect. It's a party. I need to stop obsessing about my case and just let loose." He held up a wineglass. "My one and only attempt."

"I can think of ways to make you forget about work that have nothing to do with alcohol." *Holy fucking shit, you did not just go there. What the fuck are you doing? You never proposition people.*

And yet I just had. If the guy wasn't gay or interested, he'd walk away. And I wouldn't have invested much time in the relationship. Or potential relationship.

His eyes widened comically. "Okay, I wouldn't have expected you to be so bold, but I'm totally down for whatever you're offering." He tilted his head. "I haven't seen you around before. Or not that I remember. And I have to say that I'd remember you."

"I'm not really memorable."

His eyes narrowed. "You did not just put yourself down, did you? I must've not heard you correctly."

At his sharp tone, my insides melted a little. "Well..."

"Well, nothing. We're going to pretend I misunderstood, and that you were *not* putting yourself down."

I bit my lip. "It's not that big a deal. Really, I'm just an ordinary guy. Not like you." I slanted a look at him in all his put-together gorgeousness.

He stared at me. "And you did it again. Listen up, can I give you some advice?" When I nodded fast—*yes, give me whatever, in that strong, confident voice*— he eyed me more closely.

I dropped my gaze to the floor. I felt my cheeks flush, for no good reason except I wanted him to think well of me, and didn't know how to do that.

He hummed, then bent his knees to lower himself enough to meet my eyes. "You know what? Not advice. Something stronger, from me to you. Don't put yourself down again. Not just in my presence, but anytime you're thinking of making a joke at your own expense, I want you to reconsider. To remember how disappointed I would be with you."

Part of me wanted to argue that I didn't know him. Whether or not he was disappointed in me wasn't really relevant. That we'd likely never see each other again, so why were we even having this discussion?

Yet the severity in those narrowed eyes had me holding my tongue. He'd made his point. Very effectively. In a way that set up an unfamiliar warmth in my chest.

He straightened. "Are we clear?"

Obviously, he'd let the silence linger so I could process his words and figure out my next move.

"Yes, you were very clear." Boldly, I fingered a tentacle. Slowly, I worked my way closer to him.

He had every opportunity to pull away. Instead, he leaned closer.

I moved my left hand, touching his costume and sliding over to his chest. Slowly, I trailed my finger along his pecs, outlined in the spandex fabric. I loved how the purple fabric hugged his every muscle. Every sinew. I loved how he wasn't built like a brick shithouse. I was around muscle-bound men every day. They had their place. But a man I could grasp and hold on to? Yum.

"What's your name?" He pitched his voice low.

His words washed over me. I somehow expected a slender guy to have a higher pitch, and each time, his bass tones made me shiver.

"Foster." I waited for the question or comment about my name, but none came.

He merely grinned. "I'm Arnav. In Sanskrit it means *ocean*. In Arabic, it means *rabbit*."

"As in, you like to fuck like them?" I offered a coy smile. *Holy fuck...who are you, and where have you been hiding for the last forty-five years? If you'd been nearly this brave before, think of all the guys you could've fucked.*

Maybe.

But they hadn't been Arnav. Something about him made me want to be honest about who I was and what I wanted.

Arnav's eyebrow arched as he barked out a laugh. "Foster, I think I like you."

"Enough to, uh...?"

"Fuck?"

I nodded eagerly.

"I think that can be arranged. I happen to know where Quinton's spare room is, and I haven't seen anyone else sneaking upstairs. I'll go first, and pretend I'm using the upstairs bathroom. You wait one minute and follow me up. First door on the left."

The monumentality of what I was about to do hit me hard. I was about to go to a virtual stranger's bedroom with a different virtual stranger. Quinton had invited me to the party after I visited one of my guys who'd been in the hospital for a couple of weeks—not related to work, thank God. But Bert was a nice guy who was estranged from his kids and who didn't have friends. I visited to try to keep his spirits up.

Quinton was a nurse who had spent extra time hanging around Bert's room. That boisterous personality was just what Bert—and I—needed. When the man extended an invitation to me for his Halloween party, I boldly said I'd come.

The nurse had shared that he was queer—unabashedly bisexual.

Stepping out of my comfort zone was a big deal for me. Something I was ready to make myself do.

This once.

And now there might be actual fucking? How sweet was that?

After Arnav put his wineglass on the fireplace mantel, he headed upstairs.

Surreptitiously, I glanced around the room.

No one appeared to have noticed. I spotted a lumberjack—with a beard I assumed was real—a maharajah, a harlequin, and a vampire. Count Dracula was a handsome Black man whose skin tone nearly matched my own. Attractive, but not really my...type? Did I even have a type? I'd dated so few men, and could find nothing they all had in common—except kindness. Usually displaying that kindness in letting me down easily.

I pressed my hand to my belly. Like that would somehow indicate I had to piss.

To my relief, no one paid any attention.

I slipped up the stairs and headed down the hallway to the correct door, which stood ajar. I pushed it open and saw Arnav.

He leaned against the bed with his hip cocked, his zipper undone, and his burgeoning erection pushing against his cotton underwear. He'd turned on a lamp beside the massive bed, and the glow put his face in shadow.

Then he flashed a grin, and his white teeth were on full display.

I pushed the door shut as quietly as I could. Damn, there was no lock. I only hesitated a moment. I wished Quinton's music was louder, but he kept it at a nice low hum—background noise folks could talk over. Not very helpful to mask whatever we were about to do.

Slowly, I advanced toward Arnav.

He grinned. "Kissing first and then more, eh? I found some tissues that we can use to lessen the mess, but I intend to make you come. In my hand or in my mouth...I don't give a shit."

I swallowed. "Do I get to give you a blow job?" I hadn't figured we'd be doing anal, despite the fact we'd discussed fucking, phew. I hadn't even bothered to bring a condom.

"Oh, I was hoping you'd say that." His grin revealed those perfect white teeth again.

Boldly, I advanced. When he took me in his arms, pulled me flush against him, and pressed his mouth to mine, my heart sang.

His tongue invaded my mouth immediately.

I reveled in the taste of him even as my half-hard cock brushed his.

He rumbled his obvious approval. He slid his hands around to my back, down to my ass, then pulled me close. Quickly, he ground against me.

I ground right back. My cock was now fully erect, and any kind of friction helped tremendously. That pressure wasn't enough, though. Never enough. I pulled back. "Can I blow you?"

A small sparkle lit his eyes in the dim light. "You bet.

As graciously as I could, I eased to my knees. Years of heavy labor meant they cracked on the way down. And twinged when I knelt on the laminate floor. Fuck it. I wanted a taste so bad that my saliva glands worked overtime. I slid his pants over his slender hips and lower still. Then I gently eased his underwear down.

His cock sprang free.

I angled my mouth so I could lick a drop of precum.

He moaned.

I licked around his crown, and then slowly sucked him into my mouth. To my relief, he didn't thrust. Instead, he rested his gentle hands against my scalp, slowly stroking me as I sucked him nearly down my throat. I knew when to back off and breathe and when to suck deep again.

And so I did.

He stroked my short hair as I pushed him higher and higher. Helped him chase that orgasm as best he could.

All while my cock ached.

Murmurs from the hall had me rocking back on my heels.

Arnav yelped.

I might've used some teeth.

Oops...?

The voices moved away.

Arnav groaned. So softly that I barely heard.

I snagged his cock, eased it into my mouth, and resumed my sucking. The longer I was with him, the more pleasing him mattered. I didn't fucking care if someone came in—he was fucking going to climax if it was the last thing I did. If I died from embarrassment, it would be a small—and very worthwhile—price to pay.

"Jesus, Foster, you're so fucking good at this."

A low rumble I could barely hear. I kept sucking as I caressed his balls.

"I'm..." That was all he managed before he came into my mouth and down my throat.

I sucked greedily to take in every last drop. Partly because he tasted so good and partly because I worried about clean-up. He'd said something about tissues, but if I could bring him back to rights as clean as I could, then he'd be even more pleased.

He stroked my hair to the rhythm I lapped his cock. A synchronicity I rarely found.

He stilled. "Did you hear something?"

This time, with Arnav sated and only my own dick waiting, the fear of discovery was too great. My brain shouted, *get the fuck out of here.* I let his cock slide from my mouth. Gently, I tucked him into his underwear, then I got to my feet.

And I fled.

Chapter One

Arnav

The last Wednesday of the month was Master and puppy night at Club Kink.

I was all about the puppies, but less into the *Master* thing. I saw myself as a handler. Sir, Authority, Manager, Ruler, Superior, Dominant, Boss, Sire, Dad...

Just not *Master*. My grandparents had been supporters of Mahatma Gandhi, even joining him for a time in his hunger strike. In the end, they moved to the Philippines after partition. Their daughter—my mother—headed to Canada to study linguistics. She met my Indian father, they fell in love, they married, but even in this relatively liberal land, the echoes of colonialism lingered.

My doting grandparents immigrated to Canada not long after my third sister was born. I spent a lot of time with them, learning all about life in the Philippines as well as their time in India. I wanted to be the keeper of stories in my family. My grandfather died not long after that. Nani passed just a few years ago. But before they passed, they gave me a deep awareness of history and injustice that drove my aversion to the word *Master*.

Just...hard *no*.

I liked *handler*. That worked for me.

What *wasn't* working was sitting at a table watching a small group of puppies in a circle chatting. Several had arrived with their Dominants. I'd watched carefully and gently removed them from my list of possible pups. Approaching was tricky. Making it clear I was available to be selected was bloody hard. Possibly because I'd never made it this far in my real life before. In my fantasies? I had my own pup whom I helped train. Helped make into the perfect pup. Helped fulfill their own dreams.

Maybe even loved.

A gentle hand to my shoulder made me jump.

I turned to face Dante. I'd spoken to him a couple of times when I'd come to Club Kink on regular play nights. Telling myself a traditional BDSM relationship would surely work, I'd made my way to downtown Vancouver from my small town of Mission City. An hour's drive. A whole new world. I'd lived in Vancouver for law school, of course, but I'd been overwhelmed then as well. Happy, once I graduated, to come back to my hometown and to make a life for myself. But for this, I needed the size and anonymity of the city.

I rose and offered Dante my hand. At first, he looked like he was going to hug me, but then he took my hand. I would've appreciated a hug. Some reassurance I was doing the right thing. "Good to see you."

The manager of Club Kink offered me a broad smile. "Of course. Glad to see you, Arnav. I wondered when you might come to puppy night."

I arched an eyebrow.

He chuckled. "I was pretty sure you weren't interested in a classic BDSM relationship. At the very least, I figured you wanted to be a Daddy. Whether for a little or a pup, I wasn't one hundred percent certain."

The flinch when he said *little* wasn't something I could hide. Nothing wrong with Daddies and littles. I saw them come here often when I found the courage to show up. But I didn't want an infant, toddler, or even a child in my sub's identity. I didn't want to have to parent someone. Puppy handler, to me, was a completely different thing. I offered a smile. "Apparently you know me well."

The grin Dante offered was wide. He was a few years older than me, with jet-black hair and mesmerizing dark-brown eyes. I also was aware he was in a triad relationship with a Domme and—from how I'd heard him described—a bratty sub. I mean, great for them. Also not my thing.

"I enjoy puppy night myself." He gazed lovingly over the pups. Then he refocused on me. "My submissive Evan will be here soon. He's good at facilitating introductions. He's got a good sense for people and knows many of the pups and what they're looking for. Discreet as well. Just a good guy."

A gentle laugh escaped my lips. "You speak lovingly of him. That's heartwarming."

He shrugged. "He knew what he wanted—and that was both Master Dante and Mistress Kate. The young man can be...persuasive."

"Something tells me you haven't been put upon much."

He barked out a laugh. "Uh, no." He surveyed the room. "I know several pups looking for relationships spanning from *just for play* through to *full-time, all-in, 24/7*."

"I can't do full-time or anything like that. I work long hours and can't be worried about my pup." Even just saying *my pup* brought a little thrill. "But I do want more than just for play, I think."

Dante nodded. "Let me see what I can do. Available pups are wearing the green neon wristbands."

Ah, I'd spotted three different colors. Only now did I realize they were the stoplight colors. "Thanks for the heads-up." I scanned the group and spotted three. "Perhaps Evan can introduce me...especially if he thinks there might be a connection." *Because I need to stop thinking about the guy who got away. The guy who ran out.*

That one still stung a little.

Then, as if in thinking about Foster, magic happened, and I spotted him. He hung back in the shadows watching the puppies. I was able to discern the look of longing on his face. *Can I approach him? Would I spook him? Might I be able to figure out why he's here? Tonight?* He wasn't wearing a costume. Wasn't dressed like a pup.

And sported a yellow wristband.

Inwardly, I winced.

"Are you interested in meeting that man?"

Dante had moved closer and spoke softly. I almost couldn't hear him above the house music, which was quieter than it was on normal play nights.

"He's wearing a yellow wristband."

"That's not an answer, Arnav."

My gaze shot to Dante who was only a few years older, but who clearly had wisdom and experience well beyond his years. Running a BDSM club would, I believed, require a sensitivity and ability to read people that even surpassed my need to interpret reactions and emotions. A big part of my job, certainly, but not giving me the ability to read Foster. "Do you know him? Know what he wants?"

Dante shook his head. "He only filled out a form this afternoon. We don't require that, of course, but it facilitates the...integration...into the club if we know what a person's looking for."

I chuckled softly. "I believe mine only said *Dominant*."

"Yes, but I caught you watching the pups and handlers every time you visited. Barely paid attention to some pretty engaging play going on around you."

"Whips don't really do it for me." I tapped my chin, all the while watching Foster out of the corner of my eye. If he bolted—which I completely considered him capable of—I planned to try to catch him this time. Not to confront. Just to see if he was okay. Ask what I'd done wrong a month ago.

"How about a flogger? A way to get the pup's attention while also providing an opportunity to be gentle. I know a man who makes rabbit-fur floggers. I should give you his number."

"Email it to me?" I'd provided the club with an anonymous email.

"Of course. Now...introductions, or do you want to wait?"

"Until he bolts?" Although Foster's intense gaze focused on the puppies, his gaze kept straying to the exit.

Dante cocked his head. "You know him?"

I could've argued, but what would be the point? "We met at a Halloween party. In Mission City."

"Ah. That makes sense."

That we were at a party together or that he's from Mission City? I'd probably given the club that much information about me.

Had Foster?

Too many questions and too few answers.

"I'm not certain an introduction would..." I trailed off as I watched a young man approach Foster. A cute man with short brown hair and a dazzling smile. Oh, and a purple neon wristband.

"That's Evan." Dante whispered the words near my ear. "He's wearing a house wristband. Meaning he belongs to the house, but is open for play as long as he wants to and has permission."

I tore my gaze away from Foster, then glanced at Dante. "Does that happen often?"

He shrugged. "Evan is a popular bottom. Kate and I keep him occupied, but he has tops he played with before us who still enjoying going a few rounds with him. And he's good with new Doms who are learning the skills. I might be able to advise on technique, but Evan's good at providing the feedback of what things actually feel like. He's not a pup, so he's not here to find a handler. As I said, though, he makes others feel comfortable. Especially the new and the skittish."

Skittish was the perfect word to describe Foster.

As Evan gestured the entire breadth of the club, Foster's gaze settled on mine.

Deer caught in headlights level of panic.

"Do you want a formal introduction?" Dante was already moving around me, clearly sensing Foster's discomfort.

Evan followed Foster's stare and caught my gaze. He whispered something to Foster.

Foster, to my judgement at least, appeared to relax a fraction.

A fraction.

"Whatever you can do that doesn't spook him. I'd feel incredibly guilty if he felt he had to leave. I know I'll come back...he might not." I didn't know that for certain, but that instinct settled low in my gut.

Dante was already striding toward Evan and Foster.

With fascination, I watched the interactions between the three men.

A voice interrupted. "Are you looking for a pup?"

I turned to find a young woman with sleek blonde hair, puppy ears, and a tail protruding from her spandex suit.

"Uh, no, sorry." In the war between not wanting to be rude and not losing sight of Foster, my desire for the man across the room won out.

A low chuckle came from the woman next to me. Then she sighed. "The hot ones are always gay."

"Not always." Perhaps I shouldn't argue. I knew several heterosexual and bisexual men with impeccable résumés—kind, gentle, funny, wonderful senses of humor. Just great guys. Unfortunately, to the best of my knowledge, none were looking for a puppy.

"Why don't you just go over? You're probably scaring him with that glare."

"I'm not—"

"Oh yeah, you are." She leaned in. "Go for it." Then she sashayed away with her tail swinging.

I watched her go...because someone that forthright deserved at least a moment of my attention. Then I refocused on Foster, Dante, and Evan.

Dante raised an eyebrow.

Guessing at his question, I nodded as subtly as I could.

He gestured for me to come over.

I met Foster's gaze and searched for welcome.

After a long moment, he nodded.

Well, here goes nothing.

Or everything.

Chapter Two

Foster

What the fuck is he doing here? My mind whirled as I tried to reconcile seeing Arnav, the man who'd come in my mouth at Quinton's infamous Halloween party, here at Club Kink. On puppy night. And not wearing a stoplight bracelet. *Does that mean he's a handler? A Dominant? A Sir?*

Oh my God.

I tried to remember to breathe even as this nice young man, Evan, explained how things worked. His words washed over me as I all but stared at Arnav. The man I'd obsessed over for the past four weeks. The man I'd worried about running into and yet secretly hoped I might. But at the pharmacy or grocery store or gas station. Somewhere around Mission City. Certainly not at Club Kink. On puppy night.

Does he come here all the time? In one way I wanted to know, and in the other, I absolutely didn't want to know.

"Foster?"

"Mmm?" I glanced at the generous, beautiful, and heart-achingly young man next to me. He was probably the one Arnav was gazing at.

Because who would want someone like me? Washed up, old, with no experience and nothing to offer.

"Focus on me, okay?" Evan's voice entreated me.

I blinked at him.

"The man you can't keep your eyes off of is with my Master. Dante runs the club, as you know. He's very much in control of what happens here. If you want to meet that man and chat, that's fine. If you want to head to the puppy pile with me, that's okay. If you want to go to a private room and hang with me until the guy leaves, that's fine too."

"I think I want to leave." Everything had just become too much. As much as I'd yearned to join the puppy pile earlier, that felt wrong at this point. Again, so many young pups. No one my age. No one with knees that might not hold out. No one looking uncomfortable or out of place—two things I absolutely was.

Even as I said the words, though, Dante strode toward us.

Arnav remained where he was.

I tried to read his expression, but I just couldn't. Couldn't figure out what he was thinking. Couldn't figure out why he hadn't moved on. Several pups wore bracelets indicating interest. Couldn't Dante find someone within that selection? Someone more suitable?

Dante placed his hand on Evan's back and pressed a kiss to his submissive's temple. "How are you?"

"Well, Master, thank you." He indicated to me. "Our newest pup—Foster."

I lowered my gaze. Out of respect...and because Dante's gaze was so powerful. So...mesmerizing. So...intimidating.

"You may look."

My gaze shot to the man.

He smiled. "Your actions are appreciated." His dark eyes sparkled. "I'm here to help you. How would you like to be addressed?"

"Uh..." *Think, damn it. Come up with some words....* Yet none came. "Whatever you believe is best, Sir." *Please be that be the right address.*

His nod assured me he had.

"Pup, I have someone who would like to speak to you."

"He's expressed a desire to leave, Master. I believe we need to honor that wish." Evan glanced at me.

Dante's demeanor changed right before my eyes. "Of course. We would never hold you here. If that's your desire, Evan or I—or both—can escort you to your vehicle. You drove?"

I nodded. "From Mission City."

"Ah, that's a bit of a trip back."

"He's from Mission City." I gestured subtly to Arnav.

"I believe he will be discreet, if that's what you're concerned about. But I can speak to him after you've left."

Why are you being a chickenshit? How hard could it possibly be to have a conversation with someone? A hey, how are you discussion? A proper introduction. Give him an explanation for why you ran out on him last month... I swallowed. "I suppose I should speak to him."

Dante inclined his head. "That's entirely up to you. Again, you can with Evan, myself, or both of us present. This discussion—whatever it looks like—would be on your terms. Still, you've expressed a desire to leave. Naturally, I was hoping you might interact with some pups to get a feel for what we offer here at the club, but you can always return another night. Pups never have to pay a charge."

I blinked.

Evan leaned closer. "We don't judge. Just...some submissives and pups don't have the resources."

Dante smiled. "But we also accept Dominants who might not have the resources to pay the cover charge or the membership fees. We have a rich patron who doesn't wish money to be an impediment to relationships that might develop between potential partners. Life is tough enough in this city without money as an impediment to keep people apart. If two people enjoy the same—or perhaps I should say complementary—kink, I'll do everything in my power to bring them together. Does that make sense?"

Slowly, I nodded. That was a lot of information to take in all at once. But I understood what he meant. That Arnav was looking for a submissive, or a puppy, or whatever. That he'd been vetted—for whatever that was worth—and that if I asked him to never acknowledge me, should we encounter each other again, he would respect that.

Yeah...but he's here now. You're here now. Why not take advantage of the situation? At least get a sense if you might be compatible. It sure would be easier to hook up with someone from Mission City instead of having to come into Vancouver all the time. But was proximity reason enough to overcome my nerves? To put aside that nagging voice. Mainly the one that alternated between *you ran* and *he's so beautiful, young, and smart.*

"I'll meet him. I'll speak to him." I met Evan's gaze.

"That's great." His eyes shone. "I'm always happy when puppies and handlers meet."

Could it really be that simple? Just a handler and a pup? Two people meeting in a kink club and discovering there might be compatibility? That felt way, way, way too simple.

"One word together doesn't imply anything more. We have your back, whenever you want to go." Dante eyed me with an incisive gaze.

Don't back down. You handle bigger and more intimidating guys at work all the time. Which might've been true. But there I had some authority. Here, in this space, I had less than none. Sure, the understanding was that submissives had all the power. In this moment, I felt like I had very little. Yes, I was deciding to speak to Arnav. In the end, though, he was the one who had the power to reject me.

Or I might reject him.

Or—consider this—we might like each other.

That didn't feel possible. Still, I held Dante's gaze. "I'm certain."

"Very well. I shall bring him over. Would you like privacy, or would you like company? Both Evan and I would be happy to stay if that's what you desire. Or you might prefer one or the other of us. I promise no offense if you do or do not select any of those options."

My mind raced. Advantages. Disadvantages. What message I might be sending. What message I might be receiving. Dante and Evan had their perceptions—both of Arnav and myself. So where did that leave me?

Clueless.

Like always.

I drew in a deep breath. "We've met before, and I'm certain I'll be safe." I pointed to a high-top table with two stools near the bar. "Perhaps there?"

"Excellent." Dante acknowledged my choice with a tip of his head. "Evan will get you something to drink, and I'll bring Arnav over when you indicate you're ready."

"Oh, I don't drink alcohol."

"I wouldn't recommend it anyway." Evan extended his hand. "Ulrich makes the most amazing non-alcoholic concoctions."

"Maybe just a diet cola?" My stomach clenched. "Or ginger ale?"

"Yes, ginger ale is a good choice." Evan clasped the hand I offered him. "I'll take care of him, Master."

"Yes, I believe you will, my good boy."

Evan visibly preened under the praise, his smile widening.

What would it be like? To be so adored? Or to so adore someone? I wanted to believe I might meet that special someone, but that felt more like an impossible dream. Still, I let Evan guide me over to the bar. He secured me a ginger ale and waved off my attempts to pay. "On the house."

I frowned. "Surely at some point I need to spend money."

His expression became contemplative as his smile slipped. "There are ways we can happily take your money. But tonight—your first puppy night—I don't want you to be thinking about expenses, owing anyone, or how to be egalitarian. It's your turn to be a little selfish. To ask for what you'd like. To make sure we find you the best handler possible. It's okay if Arnav isn't that person. We'll have plenty more puppy nights in the future, and I promise we'll find you someone."

The words *washed up* and *too old* came to mind. I held them in, though. Evan didn't need to hear my insecurities. I'd made it this far...perhaps I could find a way to overcome my issues. Perhaps...but likely not.

Dante strode over with clear purpose with Arnav by his side.

Evan encouraged me to sit in a chair. That would mean I didn't have to greet Arnav in a submissive way—we were meeting as equals.

Still, when the moment came, I bowed my head in deference.

"Such a good pup." Dante's words carried what I perceived as a genuine pleasure.

"Yes."

At Arnav's agreement, my gaze flew to his. I sought some kind of clue as to how he felt. Was he holding a grudge? Did he genuinely understand why I'd done what I'd done? Most importantly, could he see past my exterior?

"How do you wish me to address you?" His dark-brown eyes shone with...a touch of mischief? Remembering that the tryst upstairs during Quinton's party had very much been his idea, I sought the inner scamp who'd gone along with the idea and who had delivered a blow job.

Heat raced to my cheeks. Spotting a blush on my cheeks given my color was difficult—but not impossible. "Foster would be...preferred."

"Of course." His smile flashed with those perfectly symmetrical white teeth. "I would offer to buy you a drink—"

I protected the ginger ale Ulrich had just delivered. "I don't drink alcohol." I met his gaze and determinedly willed him to understand. I had very few hard limits in my life—but alcohol was certainly one of them.

"Then I won't either. Good to have a clear head for our discussion."

Doesn't he mean negotiation? Isn't that the right term? I just didn't know. *Should've done more research.*

"Very well." Dante turned to Arnav. "What can I have Ulrich bring you?"

Arnav gazed at my drink.

"Ginger ale." *Don't be defensive.*

"Perfect. I'd love one as well." He nodded to Dante, then joined me at the table.

Evan pressed a hand against my lower back in unspoken support.

Dante and Evan departed.

Ulrich delivered Arnav's drink.

Then I was alone with the man to whom I owed a big explanation.

Chapter Three

Arnav

Foster's nervousness was so painfully obvious that my strongest instinct was to reach out and reassure him. To figure out what made him so uptight and do everything possible to alleviate that pain. I was very much a problem solver. And good at putting skittish people at ease. Foster, though, was beyond my easy talents.

He sipped his ginger ale.

I decided to speak first. "I'm surprised to see you here. Happy...but surprised."

"You want to know why I ran."

I blinked. "Well, I was more concerned about how you're doing. Perhaps what you've been up to since we were last together."

"And why I'm here tonight."

After a moment, I tapped my glass lightly with my index finger. "Yes, to all of that. Or none of it. Whatever you're comfortable—"

"Why are you here?" His eyes blazed dark in the club's low lighting.

Bold choice.

I like it.

Unless his audacity was only because of nerves.

I cleared my throat. "Are you asking why I'm here on puppy night or why I'm an...alpha?"

He cocked his head.

"Dominant. Handler." I swept my hand through my hair that was in definite need of a haircut. "Anything but *Master*. That works for Dante and Evan. I think it's brilliant—for them. I...have other preferences."

"Alpha?" He rolled the word around in his mouth—almost as if tasting it. Trying it on for size.

"What term would you prefer?"

"Honestly?" He scratched his nose. "I've never thought about it. Honestly." He repeated the word as if desperately needing me to believe him.

"Well, when you've been in other relationships—"

He shook his head violently.

I wanted to ask—did that mean there hadn't been any other relationships or that he wasn't willing or able to discuss them with me? To buy myself some time, I took a sip of the ginger ale. I hadn't enjoyed the drink for a long time, preferring water or a smoothie when on the run. I rarely indulged in booze. A few doozies of parties in my early university days and I decided the lack of control wasn't something I enjoyed. Plus, Mama would've been unimpressed with me making an ass of myself. So I chose to swear off alcohol and had embraced a healthy lifestyle, hard studying, and career success.

"Apologies." Foster dropped his gaze to the table. "You may ask anything you wish."

I frowned. "Foster?" I said the word as an entreaty.

After a long moment, he met my gaze.

"You have the absolute right to never answer any of my questions. I ask them out of curiosity. Or to see how you're doing. Checking in with you. But responding is never mandatory. You have a right to keep private whatever you choose to. Are we clear?"

He bit his lower lip.

The move made him so impossibly adorable, I wanted to wrap him in a big hug. To ease his clear anxiety. To soothe whatever made him so visibly vulnerable.

"I..." He swallowed. "I didn't believe I had a choice."

Didn't believe...

So he'd been in a relationship and hadn't been given his autonomy, or he was trying to sort out any potential relationship with me. I shoved down the desire to seek clarification. "Tell me, Foster, what can I do for you?"

He blinked. Several times.

Clearly my question confused him.

"I..." He scratched his cheek. "I'd like to be a pup."

"Ah." *Okay, so that answers one question.* "Is that why you're here tonight?"

He nodded.

"Can you tell me what happened? In the past?" Because clearly something had.

After a long moment, he shook his head.

"I accept that. I hope one day you'll trust me enough to share with me, but if that day never comes, I won't be upset. Do you understand that?"

"I'm not a stupid man—"

"I never said you were."

"—but some people look at me and assume that I'm dumb."

"I don't think I like those people."

He frowned.

I motioned for him to continue.

"I have a decent job. But stressful at times."

"Truly, Foster, I understand."

"You're a lawyer."

"An important job at times, to be certain. I definitely keep busy."

"I'm just a construction foreman. My job's complicated. Challenging, but in very different ways from yours."

"Not my area of expertise, that's for sure." I resisted the urge to grab his hands. "We have other things we can discuss. Things that don't make you unhappy." I held his gaze. "I will never think less of you for either your employment or your desire to be a pup."

"Or my skin color."

"Especially because of your skin color." Rage bubbled with me. That he'd faced racism angered me beyond belief. I'd faced it as well, of course, but as a lighter-skinned Indian man, perhaps not as much. As much as I wanted to wrap Foster up in a huge embrace, I couldn't be certain that was what he actually wanted. Actually needed.

"That's, uh, good then." He ran his fingernails along his scalp.

Was this nervousness? More questions I didn't have answers for. "What do *you* want, Foster?"

He met my gaze with bleak eyes. "To not be alone."

"And I'm looking for someone special as well. But why don't we start simple? I'm always looking for friends—"

"Right." He scoffed.

I grinned. "I come across as having friends, do I? I do, to some extent. Everett, Quinton, August, and by extension, his husband Julian. I have acquaintances like Maddox and Ravi. But true, deep, and abiding friendships? Not so many. I've been focused since I was a kid on becoming an attorney and then, once I passed the bar, I've been obsessed with establishing my practice." I offered up a sheepish smile. "And my birth family has a habit of dominating all my free time—what little of it there is. They're...persistent."

"Sounds nice."

No missing the pain in that tone. Something I'd need to ask about later. Again, I resisted the urge to reach out.

As if sensing my thoughts, he moved his hand closer to mine.

"Do you want to hold my hand?" Said as casually as possible, as if the answer didn't matter. All the while, it meant everything.

"That feels...forward." He ducked his head.

And I resisted the urge to tip his chin so our gazes met. "Foster?"

He did gaze up.

"There is no right or wrong in this situation. You need to do what feels right for you. I have the right to decline physical affection—as do you. I'm hoping, even if we don't...get together...that you'll always choose to be around people who respect that."

"Everyone seems to." He scratched his scalp again. "Quinton asked first. Man, is he ever liberal with his affection once you say yes."

I laughed. "Yes, he's that. Once you're in Quinton's orbit, you're just kind of pulled along for the ride—no matter how you feel about it." I tilted my head. "How do you feel about it?"

He bit his lower lip. "At first, it kind of intimidated me. It's been a long time since I received...any kind of physical affection. Guys on the construction site aren't prone to *hugging it out*."

"No, I suppose not. To their detriment. Human contact, specifically skin-to-skin, is critical for well-being."

"So if we held hands, it would be good for my health?"

I caught a gleam of amusement. "Exactly what the doctor ordered."

"I don't think Dr. McCauley had this in mind." Still, he slowly slid his hand toward me.

I met him halfway.

Our fingers touched.

After a moment, I encircled his large-and-callused hand in my slender-and-soft one. The contrast made things really obvious. He worked with his body while I worked with my mind. Clearly his work had elements requiring thought, initiative, and likely some form of calculations. But while he put his body to use on a regular basis—as exemplified by his exquisite physique and visible muscles beneath his button-down shirt—I worked out by walking while listening to legal scholars' debate on podcasts.

I clasped his hand tightly. "Will you have dinner with me? Just two guys hanging out? Nothing special? No pressure?" Except with him, the dinner would be special. It couldn't help but be. I still didn't have an answer as to why he'd run from me last time, but that almost didn't matter.

Almost.

"Dinner?" He might've squeaked that.

"Well, neither of us drinks..." Him more than me, but I certainly didn't need alcohol to enjoy myself. "We could go to the Springs, which is pretty casual. Stavros's Greek Restaurant is easygoing. I mean, there's Fifties, which is super friendly." I enjoyed the diner and often snuck there for some truly Canadian food. A bit away from the Indian cuisine my family prepared and preferred.

"Fifties is a favorite amongst my crew." Again, he bit his lower lip. "I think...how about Stavros's?"

"Tomorrow night? Thursday's often busy, but I'm certain I can get us a reservation."

He held my gaze for a long time. "Tomorrow night sounds great."

"Perfect. Can we exchange numbers? In case anything happens to either of us."

We exchanged numbers, enjoyed a bit of inconsequential talk about Mission City, talked about my work on a recent case—not my choice, but he insisted on understanding a bit of what I did—and then he yawned.

"Sorry. I'm up at five-thirty."

"Ah, then perhaps we should call it a night. Or might coffee help?"

He shook his head. "Coffee at this hour would keep me up all night."

"Then yes, perhaps we should go." I used *we* because I had zero interest in staying without him. I didn't want to meet other pups. Foster had me completely enamored. Intrigued. Curious.

When we rose, Dante made his way over.

More inconsequential chitchat. Nothing about pups. Nothing about coming back. Either together or separately.

"I'd feel much happier if I can follow you home and make sure you arrive safely. You can, of course, say no." I didn't know how this would be taken. I could be overbearing and too much at times. And for all I knew, Foster might have dealt with a stalker in the past. Or someone who wouldn't leave him alone. Still, he was clearly exhausted, and watching out for him was an instinct I couldn't suppress.

"Yeah, that would be okay." He yawned again. "Sorry."

"Nothing to be concerned about." Dante offered him a smile. "Maybe check in with Evan or me tomorrow?"

That was a good idea. Both so Dante had proof I wasn't a stalker, and also Foster clearly needed to keep in contact with someone from the club. I always encouraged my submissives to cultivate friendships with other people with similar interests. So they'd feel comfortable speaking up if I was doing something that made them unhappy.

To my pleasure, Foster hadn't groused about what could be perceived as intrusiveness.

Only as I drove home, did I take in the magnitude of the evening.

And when he pulled into the driveway of an adorable little house on Fourth Avenue, I waited until he exited the car, waved to me, and headed inside.

I let out the breath I'd been holding. I still couldn't be certain he'd show up the next night, but I had a good feeling. Of course, my *feelings* had failed in the past.

Well, this will be interesting.

Chapter Four

Foster

I had to force myself not to drum my fingers on the bench in the restaurant lobby. *What the hell was I thinking? Agreeing to go out with someone I barely know? Is this a date? He said something about friends—*

I didn't even have the opportunity to finish that thought as Arnav strode in and greeted me at the entrance of Stavros's. To my relief, he just waved. To my regret, he didn't take my hand or place a kiss on my cheek.

Regret is totally nuts because you're kind of not out. And you're not certain whether he is or not either.

"Good evening, gentlemen." Stavros greeted us as he came from somewhere inside the restaurant. The restaurant bustled—clearly busy for a Thursday night. Or was it because we were so close to the holidays? Or maybe he was busy every Thursday night. Or every night for that matter. I tended to come by myself on quiet Mondays.

"Stavros, lovely to see you again." Arnav grinned. "Is our table ready? If not, we can wait—"

"Of course it's ready." The robust man chuckled, his face lighting up with obvious delight. He snagged two menus and guided us into the restaurant.

We wound our way through the floor, and I didn't spot a single empty table until we arrived at a booth in the back corner.

Arnav patted the restauranteur on the back. "Perfect. Right down to the candles."

"Only the best for you." Stavros grinned. He caught what was clearly an inquisitive gaze on my face—what with the furrowed brow and general confusion. "Someone tried to sue me, claiming the food made them sick. Your friend—" He gestured to Arnav. "—saved my restaurant. So he gets free food for life."

Arnav gaped. "Uh, no. I appreciate the gesture, but I cannot accept gifts from paying clients."

Now, I was ninety-nine percent certain that was bullshit. Public officials? Sure. Lawyers who just saved their clients heaps of money. Yeah, I couldn't see it. But then what did I know about the legal profession? Still, I respected Arnav not wanting to take money or even gratuities from someone. He struck me as very forthright.

Stavros narrowed his eyes. "If I look this up, you're telling me I'll find that in the lawyer's handbook?" His accent got much heavier.

Arnav smiled. "I'm certain you have better things to do with your time. I've been very busy today and barely had time to stop and drink. Perhaps a water and a diet cola?"

The man eyed his lawyer for just another moment before shaking his head. He turned to me. "Can I get you a glass of wine? Beer? Mixed drink?"

"Diet cola would be great." I offered my widest smile, even as my insides twisted.

"Lovely. Timothea will be here in a moment."

"Perfect." Arnav indicated I should sit.

Which I did. To my relief, he sat as well.

Stavros headed off and I let out a breath.

Arnav caught my gaze and smiled. "He's...a lot to deal with."

"He must've been an interesting client." I snagged my menu, but didn't look yet. I wanted to study Arnav's face as he revealed—or didn't reveal—what had happened. What had brought him into Stavros's territory?

My date fingered his menu. "I can share some of it. A patron claimed they got food poisoning from the restaurant and said the salmonella made them violently ill."

"Oh."

He waved me off. "Trust me, I truly hoped the claim wasn't true. Maybe that was Pollyannaish of me, but my family has been coming here for years. My sister proposed to her husband here."

That took me a moment. Naturally women could propose to men. I just didn't know any who had. On the other hand, I didn't hang out with many women, and the guys I worked with didn't generally share their engagement stories.

"I did some digging and discovered this couple who made the accusation had tried the same thing before. And succeeded. Nearly drove a small restaurant in Invermere out of business. I suppose they thought they'd gotten away with it once and they might as well try again. Easy payday. I'm certain they didn't think I'd dig that deeply or cast a net through all of British Columbia. But I did. And I discovered the same doctor had written the reports for both cases.

"The lawyer in Invermere was happy to hand over everything from her case, and the medical reports were nearly identical. When presented with that evidence, the lawyer the couple had hired walked away. I handed over everything to the police, who are close to laying charges against both the couple and the doctor, and the restaurant in Invermere is suing to get the settlement back as well as their legal fees." He grinned. "Not bad, eh?"

I blinked. "Not bad? That's amazing."

A stunning woman arrived with a tray of drinks—two diet colas and two waters. Her pale-blue eyes shone as she offered a huge grin. She had her long, black hair pulled back into a ponytail. She offered us an impish smile. "Stavros is my uncle, and he said I was to treat you as VIPs."

Arnav grinned back. "Make certain we get the full bill, okay? I don't want him paying for our meal or giving a discount."

She arched an eyebrow. "You eat here, then you follow his rules."

My date sighed. "I'm not going to win this, am I?"

"Nope. Now, what can I get you? Or do you need more time?"

"I think I know what I'm having. And Arnav was telling me how he helped your uncle." I winced, glancing at him. "Unless that was lawyer-client privilege."

Timothea waved him off. "Stavros tells everyone how this man saved him."

"And it's all in the public record." Arnav offered a sheepish grin. "Except the stuff about the police, so maybe don't mention that?"

"I hope they all rot in jail." Our server held her pen poised.

"Would you be interested in the Greek platter?" Arnav met my gaze. "Greek salad, dolmades, souvlaki, calamari, keftedakia, tzatziki, and pita."

He knew all that without looking at the menu. "Uh, that sounds great." I didn't know all the foods, but I was willing to try. Tonight was the night for being brave. Going out with...a beautiful man. I still wasn't clear if we were on a date or not. Calamari was octopus, right? How hard could it be to try that?

"For two?" Timothea glanced back and forth between the two of us.

I nodded. "Yes, sounds delicious."

She snagged both our menus. "I'll bring the salad to start and then slowly bring out everything else."

Arnav offered a soft smile. "Perfect. Thank you." After she'd departed, he turned his gaze to me. "That might've been a little bold of me. You might not want—"

I shook my head. "No, I want." I sipped my cola, letting the carbonation fizz in my mouth. "I like trying new things." *Total lie.* I stuck to my routine for a reason. I liked everything in the same order all the time. I never deviated. Well, I had last night at Kink. The jury was still out as to whether or not that had been a good decision.

Well, it landed you here. So it couldn't have been all bad.

Arnav sipped his water and then cocked his head. "I wish I knew what you were thinking."

"That I don't know anything about you." *Bold. Decisive.* "I mean, I know you're a lawyer and that's about it."

He laughed. "I don't know much about you either, but I'm willing to go first." He ran his index finger to wipe the condensation off his glass of diet cola. He rubbed his finger against his thumb. "I'm Indian, as I'm certain you've figured out. My grandparents were from Punjab.

They moved to the Philippines. My mother was born there and came to Canada for university. She married my father, and after my third sister was born, my grandparents joined the family in Canada. I'm first-generation Canadian and, I will say, very settled. But I can easily reach back to my ancestors, and so I embrace many parts of my Indian heritage. Spicy foods are my sweet spot."

"The way to your heart?"

"Phaal curry is the best food ever."

I winced. "I've never had it."

"Oh." Arnav held my gaze. "Aversion to curry or just lack of exposure?"

"I'm not certain I've ever had curry." Another wince. "Pretty pathetic, eh? Forty-five years old and I've never had that. Or half the things we're eating tonight."

"I'm sorry." He appeared to consider, with a furrow in his brow. "They offer plenty of other foods. Burgers, pasta—"

"It's really okay." I didn't enjoy cutting people off, but I had to make him understand. "Tonight's the night to try new things." I stared.

He swallowed. "Yeah, okay. So maybe we can...talk?"

I glanced around, relieved to find we were out of anyone's possible range.

Timothea returned. "Two Greek salads. It'll be a bit of time before your food arrives—we're swamped. If you need it sooner, though—"

Arnav shook his head. "We won't hold the table longer than needed, but there's also no rush on the food." He looked directly at me. "We have a lot to discuss."

She grinned. "Perfect. I'll be back soon."

I licked my dry lips.

"Drink some water. Or cola."

His eyes pierced a tiny hole into my armor. I should've resented what was essentially a command. Had we been on a casual date, it might've come off as a strong suggestion. From what I now knew of him? This was Arnav giving me a taste of his Dominant side.

Obediently, I sipped. I was incredibly thirsty, so this wasn't a hardship. *I like him taking control. Choosing the food, encouraging me to drink when I'm clearly thirsty.* A flash of pain ripped through me. I used to have this and didn't anymore.

"Why did you go out last night?" Arnav asked.

I appreciated he didn't name Kink outright in public. I poked my fork into my salad. At least I'd had this before. "Uh, I thought we were talking about you. About how your family came to Canada. How you love Indian food despite being born in Canada." *See? I listen. I care. I find you fascinating.* But I said none of those things. I merely held his gaze until I couldn't anymore. I looked down at my food—organized leafy stuff with crumbled cheese and a bit of dressing. After a moment, I put it in my mouth.

The flavor hit my tongue, and I savored it. Whatever went into this was delicious. I moaned.

Arnav cleared his throat.

My gaze shot to him.

"Keep that up and I'm going to be in an awkward position." He winked.

What...? Oh. That. "You can't help a natural reaction." I grinned. I liked the idea of making him hard—especially when he couldn't do anything about it. Because I definitely wasn't sneaking off to the bathroom downstairs with him. I was too old for stall hookups.

When have you ever done that anyway? Well, that was the truth. I was the least adventurous person I knew. Except at Quinton's party...

"I'll let that comment go." He pointed his fork at me. "Something tells me you might be a handful."

"No." I ducked my head. "I'm not, really. I'm good. I can do what I'm told." I winced. "I'm not a brat."

A gentle finger tucked under my chin and drew my gaze upward.

Soft dark-brown eyes radiated compassion and kindness. "I was teasing, Foster. I'm sorry you thought I meant it as a complaint." He continued his thorough examination of me. "I like to tease...but never in a mean way. If that makes you uncomfortable, though, then I can stop." He released my chin.

I missed the contact. "I apologize." I licked my lips again.

He pointed to my drink.

Unsure how drinking was going to make my lips less chapped, I obediently drank more cola.

"Never apologize unless you've done something wrong. I'm fair. Demanding, but fair."

He barely looked like he was out of university, let alone the twenty-nine he claimed to be. "I...I'm out of practice."

"So we'll take it slow. I'm not in any hurry, Foster. Is that clear? This is entirely at your pace."

"Dolmades." Timothea placed the plate on the table with a flourish.

I eyed the green things.

Arnav offered her a truly beaming smile. "Perfect."

"You haven't tasted them." She teased back easily.

"Ah, but they're always perfect, and I'm always grateful."

Grateful. I liked that word. The man across from me radiated sincerity. If he said the food was always perfect, then I could believe him. If he said he never teased in a mean way, I could believe that as well.

Carefully, I slid two dolmades onto my plate. *I can do this.*

Arnav grinned. "You eat and I'll tell you about my six older sisters, over-protective parents, and so many nieces and nephews that I forget them all."

He was joking. I didn't have an ounce of doubt that he remembered every single one of them, their birthdays, and their favorite...toys or books or whatever. He was *that* kind of guy. Caring. Diligent. Paid attention to detail. Doting. Caring.

Still, as I figured out how to eat the slippery concoction, I sat back and enjoyed his conversation.

Somehow, the evening passed quickly. Anytime he tried to engage me to speak about my personal life, I deftly guided the conversation back to him.

Eventually he got the hint.

By the end of the night, I'd somehow agreed to have dinner with him at Fifties diner the next night.

And as I crawled into bed, I realized I still had a smile on my face.

It had been a very long time since that had happened.

Chapter Five

Arnav

I hummed to myself as I drove the back roads north of Mission City on Friday. I glanced at the clock, considered, and then carried on. My business shouldn't take long, and I wouldn't be late for my date with Foster at Fifties. I adored the diner, but didn't indulge often. My metabolism was pretty good, but high cholesterol trended through my family. My grandmother, my mother, and now both Beena and Minal. Minal was the youngest save me, so that drove home how precarious the situation might be for me. Since I didn't have any older brothers, I had no way of knowing if this was a female genetics thing or a general thing. Regardless, I wasn't going to take the risk.

The sign for Healing Horses Ranch came into view, and I turned left into the driveway. The route was a slow upward climb through thick trees which blocked any of the remaining light. When we were so close to the beginning of December, daylight was at a premium. Night came earlier and earlier. Which meant the solstice and Christmas were coming. My family celebrated the Christian holidays—something they picked up in the Philippines. We retained many Indian traditions as well. My grandmother's philosophy was expansive rather than narrow. We noted Jewish and Muslim holidays also, although we didn't partake in them. Simply acknowledged our neighbors and respected their traditions.

As I emerged into a clearing, I spotted the parking lot, the ranch house, as well as the riding ring beyond. Somewhere would be the stables where the horses resided. Healing Horses healed people with equine, canine, and traditional therapy. I'd referred a client here after she'd left an abusive marriage. First, I'd helped her seek a restraining order.

After that legal maneuver, her husband had moved to Halifax because the asshole had finally realized she was never coming back to him.

I worried he might be abusive to someone new back east, but I couldn't do anything about that. My client had thrived, and I would have no hesitation referring other clients up here.

I pulled my SUV into a spot, noting both Stanley's and Justin's SUVs.

Stanley was married to one of the therapists—Justin Bridges. Well, formerly Bridges. He'd chosen to change his name to Powers in his personal life, retaining the Bridges only in a professional capacity.

I grinned as I snagged my briefcase.

Those two are going to be so excited.

Justin had mentioned something going on here tonight. Calling ahead to say I'd be here for certain would've made more sense, but I wanted to surprise the men. Some days, my job sucked. Other days, it was the best occupation in the world.

Today was going to be one of those days.

As I exited the car, I was greeted by a *woof*. I closed my door and then headed toward the beautiful golden retriever gazing up at me with soulful dark-brown eyes. "Hello, Tiffany."

She cocked her head as if to ask *how do you know my name*?

"Well, you're not Rex."

Her gaze never wavered.

"No, she's not." A laugh came from the woman headed my way. She wore sturdy boots, jeans, a chambray shirt, and a huge smile. "I'm Rainbow." She held out her hand.

I clasped it. "You run the place."

"Okay, now I really want to know how you know this isn't Rex."

"My name is Arnav Mehta."

She snapped her fingers. "Yeah, the lawyer. I remember now."

I appreciated she didn't mention my client by name. "Know I'll likely refer other clients your way in the future."

"Well, we're always here. Avery's a great counselor." She indicated toward the house. "I'm a little cold, so why don't we take this inside? I'm assuming you're here to see Kennedy, Avery, or Justin?"

"Well, Justin and Stanley."

She winced. "Justin's busy with a client. It's...an emergency." She held my gaze.

"I'm not here to disrupt his schedule." From her expression, I gleaned this was a bad time to interrupt.

"Stanley's getting a tour of the little house we're building for my parents when they visit. Which is more than you need to know." She led me around to the back of the ranch house. She stepped onto the back deck while indicating a pathway leading to a much smaller one-story building with lights blazing through the windows. "You'll find him there. Our handyman Simeon is giving him a tour."

"Fantastic." I saluted.

Tiffany rubbed against me.

Rainbow groaned.

I cocked my head.

"Dog hair." She pointed at a huge tuft on my dark slacks and winced. "Normally she's not so forward, but she's off the clock and feeling affectionate toward everyone."

I grinned and dropped to my haunches.

Tiffany sat and faced me.

"Off the clock, eh? I understand you work very hard."

She blinked.

Slowly, I raised my hand.

She nuzzled it.

I grinned. "I think we're, like, friends for life."

She woofed.

Rainbow laughed. "You do have a way with animals."

Slowly, I rose. "I wish. I think it's specific to your dog. I always wanted one, but my mother swore raising seven children took all her effort."

"My mother, having raised eight daughters, would likely agree."

I grinned. "I have six sisters. Our mothers should meet at some point. Commiserate about having so many kids."

"Okay, some other time you'll have to tell me about having six sisters and being the only boy. You were the only one, right?"

I nodded.

"Cool. I always wondered what a brother would've made of eight of us."

"Overwhelmed, spoiled, and loved...if he was as lucky as I was." Often, I'd chafed under the weight of six older sisters who thought they knew what was best for me. Most of the time—now I was older—I just felt gratitude and, more importantly, love.

"That's so neat. I try to talk to my youngest sisters, the twins, about what it's like to be the youngest in the family. One waves me off and says it's fine while the other is...more introspective? She's also shyer, which can be dangerous with seven gregarious siblings."

I scrunched my nose. "I went to school with Sunshine."

Rainbow snapped her fingers. "Right. I forgot you were born and raised in Mission City. Lucky were the kids who were born between each Dixon sister who didn't have one of us in their classes."

"Sunshine was great. Give my best to your sister when you see her."

"Oh, she'll be here shortly. As soon as she gets off her shift at The Owl's Nest. Tonight is the Christmas-decorating party. Oh, you should stay. Join in with cider, eggnog, and general merriment."

I laughed. "Taking in random strangers?"

She arched an eyebrow. "You're not a stranger. Which practically makes you family around here."

"Well, I happen to have a date this evening." Even as I said the words, a little butterfly flapped her wings in my belly. Admitting Foster was more than just a potential friend had serious consequences. *And maybe you shouldn't have just told the older sister of the biggest gossip in town your news...?* "Uh, perhaps I shouldn't have said that."

With a huge belly laugh, she grinned. "I won't tell Sunshine. But I am freezing, and you'd better go find Stanley."

I tipped an imaginary hat to her as I did just that. I made my way along the path to the little house. When I arrived at the glass door, I knocked.

A tall blond man with a shy smile answered it.

"Is Stanley Powers here?" I asked.

The man stepped aside and gestured for me to enter.

Even as I did, Stanley strode toward me. "Is something wrong?"

"No, far from it." I glanced around, taking in the combined kitchen-and-living-room area. I spotted two doors and assumed one was for the bathroom and the other perhaps a bedroom. "Rainbow said you were here. She said Justin was dealing with an emergency."

"Yes. He couldn't give me the details, but it's not a good situation." Stanley frowned. "Why are you looking for us?"

I was glad he made the leap I was here to see him. Made things a little less awkward. "I have something to discuss with you that's pressing. Justin mentioned the party, and I figured coming here would be simpler. Rather than you coming to the office."

"Ah, it must be important—" He arched an eyebrow, almost as if asking silently if I could just say it and put him out of his suspense.

"It is." I held his gaze. "Utmost importance."

"All right then." He glanced over at the blond man with the hazel eyes and the small smile.

"I c-can leave you the keys."

"Shouldn't take too long." I didn't want to inconvenience anyone. And, truly, the news wouldn't take long. I just didn't know who this gentleman was, his relationship to Stanley, and whether he could be trusted.

"Let's take it into the bedroom then." Stanley laughed. "That sounds really bad."

I returned his laugh. "I have visited my clients in many different places." I met the gaze of the stranger. "Lawyer. Jack-of-all-trades."

"Nice to m-meet you." He gestured to himself. "Simeon."

Right. I nodded, then pulled my wallet out of the back pocket of my slacks. I whipped out a business card to hand him. "In case you ever need a lawyer. You'd be surprised at some of the clients I've cared for since passing the bar." Perhaps a bit forward. Maybe even inappropriate. But I needed more clients to build my practice and so offering up one of many business cards just made sense.

The guy tucked my card into his shirt pocket.

Judging by his jeans and shirt, he appeared to be someone working on the building. A handyman of some kind? I nearly asked him for a card. I loved working with local people, and matching work needed to competent help always gave me a sense of accomplishment. If Rainbow hired this guy, then he was clearly good at what he did.

"T-thank you."

Stanley gestured to one of the doors.

I nodded, then followed him in.

The smell of sawdust was as pervasive in here as in the main room.

I nearly sneezed, but managed to sniff my way through it.

"It's a construction site. Or just about." Stanley met my gaze. His dark-brown eyes carried worry. The man was as serious as anyone I knew—unless he was talking about his husband or their children. Then he'd light up with pure joy. Given his past, I found that remarkable. "What's going on?"

"I wanted to share the good news in person." I held his gaze. "Cherelle has relinquished custody entirely. She's signed the papers to give full custody to you and Justin. She's indicated that, if you and Justin want to, she would like you to adopt Opal."

He blinked. "I don't understand."

The Stanley Powers I knew was whip-smart and able to take in large amounts of information while simultaneously processing it. The man before me was a loving, caring foster father who was being presented with what he'd always wanted—but had never believed would happen.

I took a deep breath. "Cherelle, sadly, was arrested recently on serious charges. I just found out yesterday and arranged an interview. She drove the getaway car after her boyfriend robbed an electronics store in Vancouver. And he shot the clerk. He's facing a huge amount of time in prison. But he's fighting it and going to trial. Cherelle is going to testify, and the crown is lessening the charges against her—but she's still going to jail for a long time." I let those words sink in. "I met with her this morning. With her lawyer as well. The very-competent woman had all the paperwork drawn up, and Cherelle signed it in front of me. Now, she said if you don't want to adopt—"

"I want." Stanley pushed the words out even as he pressed a hand to his chest. "You know I want. That we want." He blinked several times. "We've wanted this since the day the social worker brought Opal to the house. But we're her foster family. As much as Angus wants to keep her as a younger sister, we've been explaining that he can't just adopt her." He rubbed his sternum. "Because Opal has a mother. A mother who was trying to go straight..." He winced. "We honestly thought she would."

Thought or hoped? Stanley and Justin were two of the best men I knew. All they'd wanted was for Cherelle to get her act together and become the mother Opal deserved. A couple of times things had looked promising. I hadn't even been aware of this arrest until her lawyer contacted me yesterday. I'd attended the meeting without telling Stanley and Justin. I wanted to know what was going to happen before I read them in. In a million years, I couldn't have predicted Cherelle relinquishing custody. "Now, there are many steps—"

"I don't care. Whatever..." His breath hitched. "She really said she wants us to adopt Opal?"

"Yes. She's witnessed you caring for her daughter for more than a year. She acknowledged she's made a series of very bad decisions in her life—the robbery obviously being the worst. She claims she didn't know he was going to rob the store." I winced. "Her lawyer didn't even believe her—which is, I suspect, why she encouraged Cherelle to plead guilty." I drew myself up a little straighter. "With two lawyers and a corrections officer as witnesses, she made it clear she wants you to adopt Opal. If you don't want—"

"Don't even say whatever you're about to say because it's a one hundred percent *yes*. I don't even need to consult with Justin because he loves her as much as I do. She's..." He took a deep breath and blinked several times. "She's our everything, Arnav. I never thought..." He paused. "I never thought I'd have kids. Then my younger brother died, and I got custody of Angus. Justin joined us and we became a family. And I learned I had so much love to give, and then the three of us talked about fostering, and shortly after we qualified, Opal arrived. Angus adores her. We've spent fifteen months cautioning him not to get too attached—" He rubbed his chest even harder and squeezed his eyes shut.

I wanted to tell him that I wouldn't mind if he cried. Clients did that a lot. Either because I was delivering devastating news or because I was delivering amazing news. Often, because I was either alleviating stress or piling on more, they did the opposite of what I expected. "Are you okay?"

"We should..." He gestured to the door.

"Of course." I followed him out into the main room.

"I can't wait to tell Justin." He came up short as we found Simeon was no longer alone. An attractive, very slender redheaded man had joined him.

Stanley glanced at me as if asking permission. "Uh..."

I gestured for him to share.

"We're adopting Opal. It's official once we sign the papers. Her mother..." He swallowed hard. "She's given up..." He blinked rapidly.

Simeon, in a moment of breathtaking compassion, stepped toward Stanley and held his arms open.

The older man fell into them. "I...was so scared. That she'd get Opal back and not treat her right."

I glanced toward the fourth man in the room.

He pointed to the door.

I nodded.

We exited.

And stood by the door.

I extended my hand. "Arnav Mehta."

"Ryan." He didn't provide a last name.

And I didn't press. Nor did I offer a business card. Now felt very much like the wrong moment. I glanced back to see Stanley and Simeon speaking in what I could only guess was an intense conversation. I shivered, as night had pretty much fallen. The gloaming just before the last of the light was extinguished brought a chill breeze with it.

"Why don't we head to the ranch house?" Ryan pointed the way.

Since I still had papers needing to be signed, I nodded and followed him.

Upon entering the ranch house, I was assailed by the scent of cider, pine, and something undefinable, but definitely festive.

"Ryan, you have to try this." Angus, Stanley and Justin's eleven-year-old son, beckoned Ryan over.

He offered me a sheepish look before heading over to join the boy on the couch.

I spotted Opal sitting in Avery's lap. The counselor was reading a book, and the young girl, whose life was about to change in ways she couldn't possibly understand, appeared enraptured.

"Arnav." At Justin's voice, I turned.

His expression of concern had me putting on my brightest smile. "Good news, I promise." I gestured with my chin that he move to the side with me. After he did, I grasped his arm. "It's a long story that I'll explain later, but Cherelle has relinquished custody. She wants you and Stanley to adopt Opal. I have the paperwork. Oof—" I had most of the breath knocked from me when Justin hauled me into a bear hug. A chuckle rose up within me, but I held it in. He might misunderstand. I was laughing because this was such a Justin way to respond.

He pulled back, attempted to straighten my jacket, then blinked, much as Stanley had. "That simple?"

"Well, sort of. She got herself into some bad trouble with the law, and the fallout won't be pretty, but it convinced her to clear the way for Opal to have a better life. There are plenty of hoops and administrative things...but yes, she's made her wishes clear." Before I could elaborate, Stanley and Simeon entered the house.

Clearly Stanley hadn't expected Justin to be out of his office, because he made a beeline for his husband.

Justin threw himself into Stanley's arms.

I deftly stepped aside as the two men embraced.

Rainbow caught my gaze, and I headed her way. "Might there be somewhere private I can speak to the men? We have paperwork to be signed." It could've waited since the courthouse was closed for the weekend, but I didn't like having unsigned documents with me. Better to do this now. "And I'll need a witness."

She nodded. "Kennedy is really the best witness. Her understanding of legal jargon exceeds my own." Kennedy was Rainbow's older sister and the owner of the ranch. The witness didn't really need to understand the documents, and they were straightforward, but Rainbow also looked like she was going to have her hands full. What with all the boxes of decorations.

"That would work."

"Great. Let's go to her office. It's the biggest. If you can, maybe you can explain it to her?" She glanced at Justin and Stanley who held hands and pressed their foreheads together.

Thus far, Angus and Opal appeared not to have noticed anything amiss. I hoped we could get the papers signed before things got chaotic.

I glanced at my watch. *I'll have to text Foster that I'm running late.*

Why had I thought this would be simple?

Happy? Yes. Simple? Far from it.

Yet I had zero regrets.

After Rainbow left me in Kennedy's office, and headed out to locate her sister, I texted Foster.

He responded immediately and said he'd head to Fifties an hour later than we'd planned.

Guilt swamped me, but I hoped he understood.

Soon, though, I was helping Stanley and Justin begin the next stage of their lives with Kennedy as their witness.

Chapter Six

Foster

He said he's been detained because of business.
He's an important person with an important job.
He's just...running late.

I checked my phone for the tenth time in the last three minutes. I'd arrived at Fifties at the precise time Arnav had specified. Sarabeth, the wonderful server, had found me a newly vacated booth.

That had been nearly thirty minutes ago, and now the line of patrons wanting seats went out the door.

I should get up and leave. Let someone in line have the booth. I considered grabbing two stools at the counter, but they were all occupied as well. *Fuck it. I can't hold up the booth anymore.* I rose and reached for my coat.

"Hey, Foster." Sarabeth came up beside me. "You don't have to go. Why don't I have the chef whip something up for you? I know you're famished."

I gazed into her pitying blue eyes. I'd asked for a table for two and had held off ordering, so clearly she'd pieced together that I'd been stood up. "I...uh..."

"So sorry." Arnav stepped around Sarabeth and planted a kiss on my cheek. "Can you believe an accident on the road had me taking a detour that led me halfway out of town and then back? I had to go over the dam and come back in the long way. So sorry." He smiled at Sarabeth. "Could I order a coffee?" He turned back to me. "You don't have to go, do you? You're not expected somewhere else?"

He came off with bravado, but I read both the apology and the nervousness in his gaze.

Does he even realize he just kissed me on the cheek? As a way of an apology, but...is he out? Am I now out? I wouldn't have thought him so careless. Or that he would slip up in such a way. Maybe he thought, because I'd invited him for dinner last night, that I was out. Or because we'd held hands in Kink that I was okay with outward signs of affection. Or maybe he was just stressed about his job and whatever had delayed him.

Regardless, I found I wasn't as concerned about it as maybe I should've been. It wasn't so much that I was hiding in the closet...I'd just never had a reason to come out. In the end, I tucked myself against him and brushed a kiss to his chin. "I'm glad you're safe. No, I don't have anywhere else to be." I tossed my coat back to the bench seat. "Why don't we sit?"

"I'll grab that coffee. I hope no one was hurt in the accident." Sarabeth gazed at him.

"Seth said not...just too much glass to risk people driving over, and the vehicles hadn't been towed away. A real mess, but nothing serious."

At Arnav's mention of Seth, I drew in a breath. I liked the young RCMP officer. A really good guy. I didn't like the idea of him standing out on the road for hours on a cold night like this. But that was me—worrying about everyone else while not taking care of myself.

"Glad to hear everyone's okay." Sarabeth pointed to the menus on the table. "You know everything in there, and nothing's changed, but I'll leave them with you in case you're looking to try something new."

Before either of us had a moment to react to her words, she was bustling down toward the front.

"I guess she's getting my coffee." Arnav removed his coat. "I really am sorry. I didn't want to stop and text, and calling felt..." He pushed the gorgeous wool into the booth. "Presumptuous?"

"It wouldn't have been." I slid in beside my own down-filled jacket. "You can always call me." *God, please let that not have sounded as needy as I think it does.*

"I'll remember that for next time." He reached over to grasp my hand, only pulling back at the last moment. "Shit." He said the word quietly enough so no one else would have overheard him. Good thing because a number of the larger booths were full of families.

I managed a smile. "I don't mind."

"Yeah, but we've never even discussed whether you're out." Again, said quietly. "I am. I mean, after Meenakshi found my stash of gay porn when I was twelve—"

"Twelve?" I might've whispered that forcefully. I couldn't fathom.

He grinned. "Yeah, I was a precocious kid. She told my parents, who sat me down. We spent more time on the pornography issue than the gay stuff. I think they already suspected, and although my mom was a little distressed that she wasn't likely to get biological grandchildren from me, she was happy to know I was an okay kid. By then, Samara had a couple of kids, and several of my other sisters were clearly headed in that direction. Who knew Minal, the youngest, would have six by the time she was thirty-six? All that stress."

"All boys, right?" I was taking a bit of a risk, but I really had tried to pay attention last night when we'd been talking.

"Yeah." His grin widened. "You remembered."

"A coffee and another hot chocolate." Sarabeth offered me a warm smile. "On the house."

"No way." Arnav shook his head. "Everything's on me. We're celebrating, and I'm making up for being late."

I had to try. "That wasn't your—"

He held up his hand. "I insist."

Except he'd paid last night. After a tussle with Stavros over the bill. In the end, he'd accepted a discount and left the difference in a tip for Timothea.

Sarabeth glanced back and forth between the two of us. "You two are adorable."

"Still new at it," Arnav pointed out.

She grinned. "There's a lot of that going around."

Before I could ask what she meant, she pointed at the menus.

Right. She's super busy. "I, uh, will have the ham-and-cheese omelet with sourdough bread."

"I'll have the spaghetti and meatballs with garlic bread." Arnav handed her the menus. "Because I feel like living dangerously tonight."

Huh? Oh, did this have something to do with the cholesterol issue he'd mentioned last night? I should've done more research about it, but I'd been slammed at work and then had raced home, showered, then headed here.

Boldly, I reached out to take his hands. "Okay, so what happened today? Or what can you share?"

He flashed white teeth with his beaming smile. "I delivered the best news to two of my clients."

"That sounds great. Does that happen often?"

"Well, sometimes. I'm usually a defense attorney, but sometimes other stuff comes up. I defended a woman about three years ago. I secured probation. She offended again. More probation. Unfortunately, she did it again. Meanwhile, she's got a young kid, and I'm getting increasingly worried about that kid. I don't see any signs of abuse, but with the third strike, the judge sends my client to jail, and her kid goes into foster care."

Oh God. Anything but that...

"I knew the social worker, and she let me know the child had been placed with this really great queer couple." He sipped his black coffee. "I kept in touch with them on behalf of my client, and everyone sort of hoped for a reunion." I winced at "hoped for." "She got out of jail and said she needed time. She also let me know she didn't need my services anymore. I figured she was good, and as long as she kept to the terms of her probation, everything would work out."

"But they didn't."

"No." He tapped his index finger against the worn Formica of the table. "Two weeks ago, she got arrested. I won't say where or for what. That's not really important. She has a new lawyer now and wanted to see me today."

My gut clenched.

"Long story short? She relinquished custody of her child and has asked the gay couple to adopt the kid."

For the first time, I noticed he hadn't gendered the child. And had been quite generic about *gay* parents. I would never, not in a million years, share what he was saying to me.

"I shouldn't be telling you all this." He winced.

As if he'd read my mind.

"I won't tell anyone." I squeezed the hand I still gripped. "You're happy. I get it. No one else heard."

The joint was hopping, the music was loud, and we had to huddle close even to hear each other.

"Still..." He held my gaze.

I stared at him "I'm a safe place for you, Arnav. You understand that, right? I mean, you hold my secrets about, you know—"

"I would never—"

"I know. And now you know I'd never."

Slowly, he nodded. "Yeah, okay."

I held his gaze. "So you've made some people very happy today?"

"You have no idea. Truly, just...I can't even express how happy they are. Pure joy, you know? What they've always dreamed of. Wishing the circumstances were different, of course."

"Of course. We all hope for the best, but sometimes that just isn't in the cards."

He cocked his head.

Oh shit.

"Spaghetti with garlic toast." Sarabeth put the plate before Arnav as he leaned back.

We dropped hands so I could do the same when she put the omelet before me.

"You guys need anything else? Parmesan cheese?"

We shook our heads.

"Great. Flag me down if you do." And then she was off again.

"Foster—"

"Eat your food before it gets cold." Even as I said the words, steam rose from his plate of pasta.

"Foster—"

I let out a sharp breath as I met his gaze. "Not now."

"Okay. But maybe later?"

I wanted to shout abso-fucking-lutely not. But something in those deep dark-brown eyes had me hesitating. Could I deny him that? The secrets I held most closely to myself? The shit I never shared with anyone? I just didn't know the answer to that. "Maybe. Some other time." I'd try for never, but I suspected that was too long of a time to hold up my defenses. I took a tentative bite of my sourdough bread.

Arnav dug into his spaghetti as if he hadn't eaten in a month. Yet he'd packed in a huge amount of food last night. Maybe he'd skipped a couple of meals today? Or maybe he just had great metabolism? I didn't. Nearing fifty wasn't sitting well with me. I didn't feel that old, even though I knew I was. I kept my hair super close cropped, but eventually those silver strands would appear. I'd already found a couple on my chest and another couple in my whiskers when I let shaving lapse for the weekend.

"You're not eating." Arnav pointed to my food. "Is there something wrong?"

I shook my head. "I don't like super-hot food."

"Right. I think you said that last night."

I smiled. "I should clarify. I don't eat a lot of spicy food, *and* I don't enjoy foods that are super-hot in temperature. I always let my food cool a bit. Sarabeth's used to it. She no longer asks if there's anything wrong." Which was precisely what he'd done. Crap. Now I sounded defensive.

"Is that why you haven't drunk your hot chocolate?"

"Pretty much." I sipped it now. "Perfect."

"Ah." He grinned. "I order my coffee extra hot, eat my food the second it's out of the oven, and always request extra-spicy."

"Well, I'd say we couldn't be more different." Which left me with a pang. If we were incompatible with the little things, how might we cope with the big things?

He cocked his head. "Different's good. I don't want a replica of myself. I have some super annoying habits I wouldn't want to live with."

I laughed. "Okay, like what?"

"Like I'm a sucker for rom-coms and always cry at the breakup moment, even though I know the couple is going to get back together."

I couldn't envision him crying over anything. "Well, I cry during sad movies."

He eyed me. "*Old Yeller*?"

I blinked. Then narrowed my eyes. "You did that on purpose."

"I've never seen the film, but Samara said when she was a kid, the adults still thought the movie was a kid's movie. I looked that up. Showing that to a child is, like, child abuse."

That had been as true back then as it was now—but I wasn't going to share that with him. "Little Orphan Annie."

"Oh, good one. Or *Anne of Green Gables*. When Matthew dies."

Again, I blinked. "No fair. I grew up on the Megan Follows. And I remember when Jonathan Crombie died. That was super sad. I mean, the guy was just forty-eight. And gay. He only came out later in his life..." *Kind of like me.*

Arnav's eyes widened. "Okay, that I didn't know. Makes me want to google him."

"And Colleen Dewhurst died tragically as well."

"I see a rabbit hole of research appearing."

I pursed my lips.

He smiled. "Okay, maybe not. Although I wouldn't say no to a rewatch. Pooja made me watch when I was a kid. Like, she's eleven years older than me, and forcing me to watch something that she wants to make me cry. But I'm stoic. Now, Julia Roberts and Hugh Grant? Every time."

"Huh?"

"Notting Hill." His eyes widened. "Oh my God, you haven't seen *Notting Hill*? What are you doing tomorrow night?"

Since the answer was the same literally every night of my life, I answered without thought. "Nothing."

"Great. Why don't I come over tomorrow night so you can hold me while I cry during *Notting Hill*?"

My chest expanded at the thought of Arnav coming over to my house the next night. Perhaps I should've found it bold of him to assume I would allow him into my house. Except he knew where I lived, likely how I lived, and I didn't worry. Somehow, this was right. If I'd known this was what he wanted, I would've made the invitation.

Part of me was curious as to why we couldn't go to his place, but that didn't matter. I had a private house. I lived alone. Welcoming him would make me feel good—and something assured me he understood that. I'd be comfortable in my own home. With my familiar things. In the place I felt most safe. He wasn't invading—he was adding a new element of comfort.

I found the courage and offered a wide smile. "I can't wait."

Chapter Seven

Arnav

I didn't normally invite myself to other people's houses. That was rude.

Inviting them over to my place was...awkward.

Mostly because I still lived in my parents' home. Yes, I had my own suite in the basement which was as luxurious as many people's apartments. Yes, I had my own entrance and a lock between myself and the rest of the house. But also yes, my family regularly knocked on that door to make sure I was *okay*.

Especially Rashmi who had moved back into our family home after her divorce.

I wasn't clear on the entire situation. She used to talk about having a large family. But she'd never had kids. She used to talk about adoring her husband. But for a long time now, those hadn't been sentiments expressed. She'd attended family functions alone for the past year or two—always making excuses for the guy. Then, one day out of the blue, she moved home.

We didn't talk about it. Well, she might speak about it with our sisters or our parents, but she certainly never confided in me.

Now she tried to mother me. To smother me. At twenty-nine, I found that a little much. Except I saw, in brief moments, her pain. So I gave her more latitude than I might have otherwise.

Meanwhile, I saved for my nest egg to buy a house of my own, and I appeased my parents who always had an excuse why I should stay.

Some of those excuses were downright ridiculous. Others were heartfelt, and I found hard to refute them. But, I'd put down my foot. I was moving out at the age of thirty. Which was on January twelfth. I'd engaged a realtor, Cadence Crawford, to start scouting properties. I had a healthy down-payment saved, a stellar credit record, and an excellent source of income, so securing financing wouldn't be an issue. I likely wouldn't be able to purchase the single-family home I wished, but that was more speaking to the cost of real estate in Cedar Valley rather than disparagement over my efforts to save.

And none of that was relevant tonight. I'd invited myself. Foster had smiled and agreed. I had my Blue-Ray copy of Notting Hill. Hopefully he had a player. If not, I was happy to pay to watch it on a streaming service.

I'd dressed down tonight. No shirt and dress pants—as he'd seen me in the last three nights. I'd opted for jeans, a turtleneck, and a leather jacket. Fashionable and not really appropriate for the biting wind whipping across downtown Mission City on this chilly night. But I didn't intend to stand outside for long.

And I didn't have to. Foster opened the door even before I had the chance to ring the bell. He stepped aside and beckoned me in.

"Hi." A little shy. A little hesitant. A lot cute.

"Hello." I waited as he closed the door behind me. The warmth permeated immediately, and I worried he might keep his house warm. In that case, the turtleneck might not have been the best idea.

"May I take your coat?"

"Certainly." I removed it and our hands brushed as he took it.

He hung it up in his front closet.

Then hesitated.

I asked, "May I kiss you in greeting, or is that too forward?" Another bold move—but I always sought permission, and I was giving him every opportunity to say no.

Another shy smile. "I think I would like it if you kissed me."

Not quite as definitive as I would've liked, but Foster had moments when he could strongly articulate what he wanted and other times when he didn't. When he almost appeared to believe he wasn't worthy of nice things. That he didn't deserve what he wanted.

Slowly—so as not to spook him—I approached. I placed my hands on his biceps and leisurely ran them up to his shoulders and his neck. Farther still, I ran them along his jaw and up to clasp his smooth-shaven cheeks. Normally I enjoyed diving in. Tonight wasn't the time for that. I lowered my head, still maintaining eye contact.

Eventually his eyes drifted shut.

I let my lips brush his. Just the lightest of touches.

He placed his hands on my chest. To steady himself? To push me away?

I wasn't certain.

So I continued. I pressed our lips together again. His were chapped and rough while mine were smooth. Moisturizer. Having all those sisters meant a rigorous skin-care regime. Probably why I appeared even younger than I was.

He grasped my turtleneck.

I nibbled his lower lip.

He opened for me.

I took full advantage, thrusting my tongue into his mouth. I meant to be gentle, but his soft pliancy had me taking full control. I levered him closer to me even as he wrapped his arms around my waist and drew me nearer. As I plundered his mouth, he moved against me, brushing his erection against my hip. Worried he might be embarrassed, I redoubled my assault on his mouth. If we moved to frotting at some point, I was totally fine with that.

He moaned, splaying his hands on my lower back and pressing our bodies as tight together as possible.

We'd gone from zero to one hundred in a nanosecond and my thoughts raced to keep up. I was happy to keep dominating this encounter, but I'd honestly just thought we'd be watching a movie. If he wanted more, I was certainly up for that. Truly, though, I was confused. He came across as a little shy. A little reticent. The man in my arms now was none of those things.

Something felt...off.

Slowly, I pulled back.

He gazed up at me with glazed and confused eyes. "What...?"

"Foster, what do you want?"

"This."

"Okay." I drew in a ragged breath and gazed into gorgeous dark-brown eyes. "But are you doing this because you want to, or because you believe this is what I want?"

His brow knit. "Are you not pleased?"

Aw shit. "I'm very pleased. I'm enjoying myself. But that wasn't the question I asked you."

He drew his lower lip through his teeth. "I don't know what to say."

"Say the truth. I only ever want the truth from you. Is that clear?" I might've been a little harsher than I would've been otherwise, but I didn't want there to be any confusion.

"Are you saying I did something wrong? That I wasn't good enough?" His voice quavered.

Confirming my suspicion. "Foster, you were perfect. I enjoyed kissing you. But I need you to understand that I don't expect a kiss."

"And you think even though I said yes, I didn't really want one."

"I think you felt an obligation." Which, whether I was right or wrong, meant a lot to unpack.

He held my gaze for another moment before looking away. "I enjoyed it."

"That's great."

"I might want to do it again."

"Sounds lovely."

"But..." He swallowed. "My former owner...boyfriend...whatever..." He sighed. "I wasn't good enough for him. He tired of me. Nothing I did was ever good enough." He met my gaze. "I don't think I'll be good enough for you."

Wow. Shit. "I appreciate your honesty. I think we need to have a dialogue about this."

His face fell.

"Perhaps after the movie? Or another night?"

"Or never?" He whispered the words.

I shook my head. "I need to know where you are at. What happened in your previous relationships. I might be young, but I have a sense for people. You wear your hurt and I catch glimpses when you let your guard down. When you think no one is watching. I'm always watching. I'm also willing to give you as much space as you need."

"I don't exactly want to wallow in my failure."

I cocked my head. "Failure?" Certainly a word I didn't like—especially when spoken by someone about themselves.

"He left me. Well, more like he kicked me out. I had enough savings to rent a place. Not great, but I managed. Eventually a friend offered this place. He'd had a string of bad tenants and the place was a mess. In exchange for a discount on the rent, I've been slowly fixing the place up. Making improvements during my spare time." He straightened a little.

Finally, I broke his gaze and looked around. The space wasn't large, but enveloped me in coziness. "This place is lovely. Why don't you give me a tour?"

Slowly, a smile crept onto his face. His face lit. "Yeah?"

"Yes. And then I have to go out to the SUV because I forgot the movie."

"Why don't you do that while I get you something to drink. Do you have a preference?"

"Something warm on a cold night?"

"Coffee?"

"I think that's too much caffeine. Do you have hot chocolate?" He'd consumed several cups last night and had appeared to really enjoy them.

"Yeah, that would be great."

I caressed his cheek. "I'll get the movie."

He blinked. "Okay. I'll make the hot chocolate. Milk okay? Some people prefer water..."

"Milk is perfect."

"Great." He continued to hold my gaze. Then, unexpectedly, he went on his toes and pressed a broken kiss to my lips. Before I could react, he scurried toward the back of the house where I assumed his kitchen was.

I eyed the closet, decided I'd survive the thirty second trip to my SUV, and headed back outside.

Fat flakes of snow hit me as I darted to the vehicle. I disarmed it and yanked open the passenger door. I nabbed the cloth bag with the ten Blue-Ray discs I'd brought, slammed the door, hit the alarm button, and booted back to the warm and inviting house.

Foster greeted me with a smile and then a quizzical expression. "I thought you said you were bringing *Notting Hill*?"

I offered a wide grin as he shut the door. I held up the bag. "I did. And then I thought I should bring one other. Just in case you weren't enjoying Hugh Grant and Julia Roberts. Then, though, I got analysis paralysis."

He arched an eyebrow.

"Well..." I toed off my running shoes. "If you liked Julia Roberts, but not Hugh Grant, then I thought you might want to watch *Pretty Woman*. And if you liked Hugh, then *Nine Months* is a must. But if you enjoyed the Brit part, then you have to watch *Sliding Doors*. Gwyneth Paltrow is wonderful, but John Hannah steals the show. And if you like John, then definitely *Four Weddings and a Funeral*. Then there are all the Meg Ryan movies. She was in so many classics— *When Harry Met Sally, Sleepless in Seattle, You've Got Mail*..." I drew in a breath. "But if you like Gwyneth, then *Shakespeare in Love* and *Emma* are musts." I considered. "Well, and if you like *Emma*, then you'll love the modern retelling, *Clueless*. And Drew Barrymore has a couple of films I enjoy. I'm partial to *Never Been Kissed*. Then there's *Jerry Maguire* and one of my faves, *The Truth About Cats and Dogs*. And—"

Foster held up his hands. "Okay. Uh...breathe? That's, at last count, fourteen movies? Are you planning on moving in?" His eyes sparkled with clear amusement.

"Uh...no." I held up the bag. "I only brought ten. I figured we could ration them out over several nights. Maybe mingle in some of your favorites?"

He brushed at my shoulder. "Snow?"

I nodded. "Yeah. Not too bad."

"Is it supposed to get worse? My crew is working inside next week, so I haven't been paying as close attention to the weather forecast as I normally do."

"No idea." I offered the bag. "Perhaps you want to select?"

"Again...I thought we were watching *Notting Hill*. I even read up on the movie so I could discuss it intelligently."

Alarm bells clanged loudly. "You can say whatever you want about the movie. About any movie. Or about any subject."

He ducked his head. "Sorry."

Slowly, telegraphing my moves, I tucked my index finger under his chin and guided his gaze to me. "What is it?"

"I'm not, you know, super smart. I'm good at my job, but I don't read a lot of extra stuff. Gives me a headache."

For a moment, I wondered if he might be dyslexic. Or just found reading a lot of material overwhelming. Pretty much the opposite of me—I basically read for a living. And enjoyed reading for pleasure as well. *Be careful what you say.* I didn't want to censor myself, but I kept toeing potential landmines. Until I had a clearer picture, I needed to be careful.

"Have you had dinner?"

He shook his head. "Too nervous."

"Ah. Well, I was mired in paperwork, and before I realized it, I needed to dress to come here."

"You were doing paperwork in the buff?" He grinned. "I would've liked to see that."

I tapped his nose. "No, not in the buff. Just in some sweats. I wanted to look respectable."

"I think you'd look respectable in anything." Gently, he fluttered his hand through the hair that fell over my brow.

"I think I need a haircut." I was so damn busy that I never had time. Well, until things got critical because my hair was just too damn long.

"Your hair's perfect." He ran his hand over his closely cropped head. "Mine's always unwieldy." He winced "And I might be going bald. Definitely not a good look. I think eventually I'll start shaving it."

Another dig at himself.

Before I could say anything, though, he beckoned me to follow him to the kitchen. "I have a milk steamer. I can whip you up a hot chocolate in no time."

"That sounds lovely. Now, we haven't eaten. I'd like to treat."

Foster shook his head. "No way. You paid for Stavros's and Fifties. Tonight's my treat."

Don't fight him. Just opt for something inexpensive. "Fair enough. Honestly, I have no idea what to order. What do you feel like?"

He pulled a jug of milk out of the fridge. "I can say in all truthfulness that I don't have a preference." He poured the milk into a mug. "I've got those app things on my phone. Or I can run out to pick something up."

I gazed around the cozy kitchen.

The table and four chairs were against the back wall next to a large wall of windows.

I assumed they faced the backyard. With the darkness, I couldn't see anything.

The appliances all stood against the wall with a little island delineating the two spaces.

As I searched for some clue as to what he might want to eat, I let the informality of the space sink in. So different from my family's modern and state-of-the-art everything.

A flyer for Domino's caught my eye. "Pizza?" I asked the question casually, just as he flipped on the steamer.

"Sure." He raised his voice. "One minute, okay?"

"Yes, absolutely." I continued my perusal of the space. The appliances were serviceable, but showed some age. The countertop was chipped in several places. Nothing bad or anything. Just that this house was showing her age. Which made me curious about just how old the building actually was.

Foster turned the steamer off. He placed his hand under the mug and gingerly handed it to me. "I don't think I need to warn you that it's hot. Ye who enjoys hot drinks."

"And foods." I saluted him and took a sip. "This is perfection."

He ducked his head. "It's the steamer."

Fucking hell. "Foster?"

After a long moment, he met my gaze. And swallowed visibly.

"I told you not to speak negatively about yourself, right? You remember that?"

"Yes."

He held my gaze, but the war of emotions crossing his face had me considering my next words carefully. "I complimented you. This is a perfect cup of hot chocolate. The steamer didn't pick the right amount of chocolate powder. The steamer didn't choose the correct amount of time. Right?"

"Well...no."

"Okay. So when I compliment you on a perfect cup of hot chocolate, what should the response be?"

"Thank you. I hope you enjoy it." He said the words quickly. Forcefully.

Still, I'd take it. *Small steps.* I snagged the flyer. "Please tell me you don't take pineapple on your pizza."

I caught the small smile as he turned on the steamer to prepare his drink.

Oh well, this should be interesting.

Chapter Eight

Foster

I couldn't stand pineapple on my pizza. Ick. Gross. Disgusting. Invented by a person with seriously bad judgment.

But I did string Arnav along for quite some time. Right up until he started to order the pizza on his phone to block my pineapple craving.

I pointed out that since we'd agreed I'd pay, that it only made sense for me to place the order, and since pineapple on pizza was right up there with anchovies as a bad idea...

He wagged his finger at me for the lie.

I offered a sheepish grin. And then laughed. Honestly, laughing felt good. I'd all but admitted to him that I'd been in a bad relationship. Howard hadn't been abusive. Well, not physically. Well, not much. But he hadn't always been a nice person. He'd spent a lot of time putting me down. And so I'd internalized a lot of that.

Vivi, a woman I worked with, wanted me to see a counselor. Or a therapist. She'd even made a few suggestions. Which I'd accepted and then never called. I wasn't going to waste a counselor's time. I was fine. Feeling rejected by someone I'd believed myself in love with...but fine.

Yet, as Arnav watched me intently while sitting in the living room waiting for the pizza, I questioned that assertion. His uncanny way of reading me really unnerved me. "Uh, are we watching *Notting Hill* tonight?"

"We can do whatever you'd like." He sat on the couch with his body angled to face me. He had an arm draped over the back and sat clearly loose-limbed.

I, on the other hand, was a bundle of nerves. *Why did I think bringing him here would be a good idea? Oh, wait...he sort of invited himself.* Not that I had any objections to that. I didn't. I would've done so myself except my house wasn't anything great, and I was certain—successful lawyer he was—that he likely lived in an amazing house. Nothing like mine.

Still, after ordering the pizza, I'd given him a tour. We'd started upstairs where I showed him the renovated bathroom and the two bedrooms I'd fixed up.

He'd complimented me.

I hadn't refuted him.

Then I'd shown him the new flooring on the ground floor as well as the new cabinets I'd installed. The furniture was a little cringeworthy, and I hadn't told him I'd acquired it at the charity shop. I'd told myself reusing was good for the environment. The truth was, I hadn't had money to spare, and this place hadn't come furnished. I had splurged and bought a new bed, though. The second bedroom just had a desk and a dresser. I figured the next renters could either turn it into a spare bedroom or a nursery. This house wasn't big enough for a full family. Or at least I didn't think it should be.

My really hard work had come in the basement. When I'd arrived, it had been dank and, frankly, gross. I'd gutted everything down to the studs, cleaned everything to within an inch of its life, and then rebuilt. I was in the process of creating a third bedroom, a second bathroom, a proper laundry room, and a gaming room. The space was welcoming. The thing was also expensive to heat for just one person, so I kept it closed off and rarely went down there except when working on it.

The doorbell rang.

I leapt up to answer it. I'd expected a text letting me know the driver was on their way, but that didn't always work. As I opened the door, I found Inga at the door. She was about my age and delivered pizzas to supplement her husband's salary working at the hardware store. One night, when she hadn't been busy, we'd chatted for a few minutes. I didn't order pizza often, but I was always grateful when she delivered. "Thanks."

"Thank you for the big tip." She handed me the pizza as well as the box for garlic bread. "You staying in?"

I peered into the darkness beyond her. The pink streetlights illuminated the falling snow. "I have company."

"Oh." She grinned. "Lucky you. I just have my monsters waiting at home." By monsters, she meant three children she adored, her Havanese puppy, and her lug of a hubby.

I envied her. "It's, uh..." I jostled the food. "Not a date. I mean, not really."

She continued to smile far too brightly. "Well, enjoy your *not really* date. Snow's supposed to pick up just after midnight. Be careful, okay?"

"Yeah, thanks. I'll let him know."

Inga knew I was gay—one of the very few people in Mission City I'd confided in—so referring to Arnav wasn't a big deal. Now, since he'd kissed me on the cheek at Fifties, probably half of Mission City knew I was gay. Nothing stayed secret in this town for long.

Except my relationship with Howard. We'd been living in Vancouver anyway. A long way from the sleepy town I'd relocated to.

Yeah. That. And so not the time. "Be safe."

"I will." She headed back with her padded bag. She hopped into her car and was gone in the blink of an eye.

"Everything all right?"

I spun to find Arnav close.

"Yeah. Just making sure Inga's okay, you know? The snow's heavier and some's sticking. You might want to go soon."

"I have snow tires. Didn't she say something about it picking up after midnight? Sorry, I didn't mean to eavesdrop. I was just concerned."

His contrition appeared genuine. He didn't seem like the jealous type. But then what did I know about that? Howard had never been jealous because he'd known no one wanted a forty-something washed-up man who wanted to crawl on all fours and act like a dog.

Who does that, anyway?

The pile of young men and women who'd been enjoying themselves at Kink on Wednesday night. One of my biggest regrets was that I hadn't joined them. Or at least spoken to some about their experiences. I didn't regret spending my time getting to know Arnav, but I'd gone to get a perspective that I still felt I didn't have.

Evan's phone number haunted me. The young man had said to call so we could have a proper chat. That although he wasn't a pup, he was a submissive. That he knew lots of pups and would be happy to facilitate introductions.

"Foster?"

"Um?"

Arnav gestured to the pizza. "Would you like me to take it?"

"Yeah." I handed it to him. I needed to be more focused. My mind jumping from topic to topic to topic wasn't going to stand me in good stead. I had an attractive man in my house, and I should be doing my level best to give him my full attention. "I'll grab plates. Do you want a soda? I grabbed some diet cola in case you wanted it."

He offered a wide grin. "That was very considerate of you. You don't drink it?"

I shrugged. "Not often. I'm really a water, tea, and hot chocolate guy. Coffee first thing in the morning, but then I ease off caffeine for the rest of the day."

"Ah. I mainline the stuff all day and then struggle to sleep at night." He headed into the kitchen.

"Well, that's not good. How do you sleep?"

"By reading law-review cases. Puts me out within ten minutes every time, even if it doesn't last." He placed the pizza on the counter. "Guaranteed eye-closer."

"Yeah, I can't imagine that would be stimulating."

"No. Other things, certainly? Tort law? Definitely not."

"I thought you were a defense attorney. You do injury law as well?" I pulled two plates down from the cupboard.

"No." He opened the lid. "I stick to defense attorney with a few other things thrown in. Torts are not my jam. Hence reading them to put myself to sleep. Two slices or three?"

"Two is great." I moved to the fridge. "So mostly defense. Don't lawyers pick a lane and stick to it?" I pulled out two chilled cans of pop, then closed the door.

"Usually. I chose criminal law because I thought I wanted to be a prosecutor. Spent a summer working in the office and realized that job wasn't for me. I wasn't sold on the idea of defending people either. At law school, I had the choices of Indigenous law, business law, environmental law, or the law and social justice specialization."

"That's the one you chose." I handed him the can of pop.

"Yeah. I had zero interest in business. Indigenous law intrigued me, but I didn't see it as a good fit for me. Environmental law appealed to me in some ways, but again—not the right fit. That left social justice. Criminal law is just part of that. Advocating on behalf of clients is a bigger part. For me, anyway. So yes, I do defense work. I also try to represent those who might've been left behind." He tapped his chin. "Some of the folks I went to school with are already kicking ass and taking numbers. The ones on the business track are especially raking in decent money." He grinned. "I'm not that person. Yet." Then he grabbed his plate of pizza and his cola. "Do we eat at the table, or—"

"Living room is fine. I'm not fussy and the couch..." I did my best not to wince. "Has seen better days."

"That's fair. My stuff's a bit older, but sturdy. I'm all for taking care of things. Of not getting rid of them the moment they're out of style."

Does he think my furniture is out of style? Damn.

Except I reminded myself, he hadn't said that. That was what I'd heard—but that wasn't the same thing.

We made our way into the living room. He stood aside and gestured for me to sit first. Momentarily disoriented, I pondered. Guests sat first, right? Except... Oh. He wanted me to take *my* spot. The spot where I'd be the most comfortable. Little did he know, I alternated sides so I could make the couch last longer. Or at least that was my theory.

I chose the right-hand side and plopped down. I expected Arnav to select the chair, but he sat next to me on the couch.

He cracked his can open and took a sip.

And sighed.

I grinned. Sometimes he was so easy to please—other times I strug-gled to read him. To figure out what he wanted. What would make him happy. I also reflected on his comment about not perhaps doing as well in his job as some of the other graduates from his year. Did he resent they were *raking in decent money*? If I didn't work for a nonprofit, I could definitely be making more money...

"Are you going to eat?" Arnav held up a slice from which he'd taken a bite. "Because I understand waiting until the guest has started, but waiting until they're finished is a little awkward."

He offered the endearing grin I was coming to love so much. "It's fine." I picked up a slice. "Oh, did you want to start the movie?"

"I was going to suggest we talk some more, but yes, I think watching a film would be enjoyable."

Before he could rise, I had my cola and plate on the side table. I snagged the bag on the coffee table and rifled through it, quickly locat-ing *Notting Hill*. Serendipitously, I owned the appropriate machine, and loading took mere moments. I turned on the television and sorted out the remote. "Sorry the screen isn't bigger."

He waved me off. "I'm not into screens that are so large you can't take everything in. To me, there is such a thing as too big."

Heat raced to my cheeks, and gratitude swelled in me that he couldn't see me blush. *He wasn't talking about cock size, and you shouldn't be thinking about his cock size.* Seeing as I didn't have much experience—Howard was pretty much my one and only—I was in-tensely curious. I'd been bigger than Howard, which was the excuse he used to never bottom. More incompatibility.

The copyright screen lit, and I settled back into my seat. The next hour and a bit flew by as I took in the movie I'd never seen. Truthfully, movies weren't really my thing. I watched hockey, football, soccer, and rugby. All the British Columbia teams. Well, those were all pretty much Vancouver. I would also catch the news and, more often than not, documentaries.

A sniff caught my attention.

Both Arnav and I had long finished both our pizza and colas. Somehow, he'd moved closer to me. Or I'd drifted toward him. Regardless of who had moved first, less distance separated us than before.

I surreptitiously glanced over at him.

A lone tear streaked down his face.

I refocused on the movie. Hugh Grant was sitting with his friends as they discussed his breakup with Julia Roberts. How some thought he was right, and one thought he was an idiot.

Arnav sniffed again.

He'd said he expected me to hold him when he cried. Or hoped I would? I couldn't remember his exact words. But, in essence, he'd offered.

Before I could overthink things, I slid toward him.

He shuffled toward me, his focus still on the screen.

Some antics were ensuing about a car or something or other.

I placed my arm on the back of the sofa.

He tucked himself into my side and grasped my henley.

I pulled him toward me by wrapping my arm around his biceps and applying pressure. *God, this feels so good. So perilously perfect. How did I get to be so lucky?*

Even as I had the thought, Julia sat at a table during a press conference. And Hugh Grant arrived. And asked a question. And she answered. Then another reporter asked a question, and she answered, and all these cameras flashed, and... Yeah. That was the happy ending, right?

Nope. Then they were on a park bench and she had her head in his lap. He was reading and she had a baby bump.

Then the movie was over.

As the credits rolled, I continued to hold Arnav.

Only as the last of them ended, did he stir. He sniffed. "Uh, sorry."

"Don't be." I moved my hand gripping him so he could sit up. "I think it's sweet."

"It's something." He rubbed his face. "May I use your washroom?"

"Sure, you remember it's upstairs? Do you want dessert?"

His dark eyes lit. "Dessert?"

"I might've bought a cheesecake. I mean, you had the hot chocolate, so I figured you weren't lactose intolerant. I also have some ice cream."

"Cheesecake." He grinned. "I adore cheesecake."

"Okay." I grinned back. "I have strawberry jam, chocolate sauce, or cherries—"

"Oh God, cherries. Please, cherries."

"So easy to please."

He stilled. "Yeah, I am. I can also be demanding. But mostly free with praise and grateful for everything. I've had a good life, Foster. For me, that means paying that forward whenever I can."

I tried to discern his meaning, but couldn't. Perhaps I could just take him at his word. "I'll get the cheesecake."

He hopped up. "And I'll run upstairs."

After he'd disappeared, I sat still for a very long time. Well, long enough his footsteps on the old, creaky staircase ceased. Finally, I organized our plates and pop cans and took everything into the kitchen. I removed the cheesecake from the fridge, cut two slices, and sorted out the cherries from the tin.

By the time Arnav was back, I had the two plates ready to go.

His eyes lit. "Oh, I'm so excited. Mom prefers traditional Indian desserts. Or sometimes she'll do chocolate cake."

"What do you have when you're alone?"

He cocked his head. "I'm never...oh. Right. You mean when I'm at my place." He tapped his chin as if in contemplation. "Truthfully? I'm not really a dessert guy. Grateful when I have it, but I don't go out of my way." He nudged my arm. "So, this is the best choice ever."

That felt a little over the top, but I wasn't going to question his enthusiasm.

Chapter Nine

Arnav

We devoured the cheesecake with cherries on top while standing in the kitchen. When I suggested another movie, Foster eagerly agreed. He never hid his enthusiasm. Which meant, to my understanding at least, that when he wasn't happy, he would shut down. Give me neutral. Not be as happy.

So I needed to do everything in my power to make him happy.

Since he'd enjoyed *Notting Hill* and had enthused about Julia Roberts, I chose *Pretty Woman,* and we settled back onto the couch. This time, I ensured we were right next to each other. I even placed my hand on his thigh.

He settled with his arm next to mine.

I managed right up until the moment Julia Roberts got in the limo to head back home—alone.

Yep. Tears. I couldn't help myself. Even though I knew for certain Richard Gere would be her knight in shining armor—sticking his head out of the sunroof of the limo—I still sniffed and eventually, cried.

Cathartic tears.

Foster wrapped his arm around me and pulled me against him.

I clung to his shirt and used it to wipe my tears. Fortunately, I didn't usually have snot. Perhaps because, although I was moved, I didn't despair. I'd only had those moments of true sobbing in my life a few times. In practice, though, I'd witnessed many tears from my sisters. Beena, in particular. With all her dramatics, she could turn on the waterworks. Not that I ever judged...because she'd sure as shit tease the hell out of me if she knew I cried over rom-coms.

The happy ending came, and then the credit rolled.

Foster angled himself back so he could see my face, and he wiped a stray tear. "This is adorable. I love that you're so free with your emotions."

So much said in so few words. He obviously didn't feel he could be free with his. I doubted Julia Roberts comedy movies could bring him to tears, but how often did he feel the need to suppress his emotions? To be stoic? To hold things in?

I would work to change that if we began a relationship.

"I think I should be going."

His face fell. No other word for it as his mouth drooped.

"It's only nine-thirty. It's Saturday night. Surely, we can do one more movie? I really enjoyed that one."

I considered. "Sure. Do you have any idea which you'd like to watch?"

He bit his lower lip. "I don't have any idea."

"Well, Hugh Grant and Julianne Moore are in *Nine Months*. It's cute."

"That sounds great." He disentangled from me and rose. "I need to go upstairs. Would you like something to drink? There's more cola. I can make a coffee or a hot chocolate with my machine..." He wrinkled his nose. "But caffeine this late might not be good. I've got teas—"

"A glass of water will be perfect. Would you like me to grab you one?"

"Oh yes, thank you! I'll be back."

The enthusiasm with which he offered up his *thank you* struck me. Like he'd never been offered a simple courtesy before. At least not by someone who might be a potential partner.

I made my way to the kitchen. More and more, I felt we were falling into dating. Perhaps even falling into a relationship.

After locating two glasses, I checked the freezer for ice.

Score.

I debated whether to add them to Foster's glass just as he appeared. "Oh, perfect timing."

"Yes, to ice." He grinned. "Good call."

I put several ice cubes in each glass then added tap water. I presented Foster with his and we clinked glasses. "Okay, so we're agreed on the movie. We'd better get to watching it right away since the snow's supposed to intensify at midnight."

"I'll get you out of here before then, Cinderella." He gave me a shy smile.

"You know, I always thought she should've stuck around. So what if her ballgown disappeared? So what if the glass slippers vanished? The prince could see her for who she really was. That was important, don't you think?"

He tilted his head, clearly in contemplation. "Sure, but when he does meet her, and finds her in those circumstances, he accepts her readily."

"Okay, but the Grimm version was, well, grim. Chopping feet and some shit." I rummaged in the bag. "Oh, Drew Barrymore starred in *Ever After.* I love that movie."

"Another nineties rom-com?"

"Well...sort of. Less comedy, but still really sweet. Another night."

"You know, someday I want to see this clearly vast array of movies you've collected."

Tires screeched in my head. "Uh, sure." *Like when I move out and get a place of my own...* Here I was, trying to impress him, and I still lived in my parents' basement. I might've been a lawyer, and properties might've been expensive, but it still didn't sound all that impressive.

He considered me, staring openly.

"What?"

"You're not..." He shook his head—as if shaking off the thought. "Movie."

Since I didn't feel like opening up about my living arrangements, I nodded and we headed into the living room. Again, we settled to watch the movie. This time, I snuggled against him right away. I preferred to be the Dominant in relationships, but I was super happy to yield the role of comforter while I watched my movies.

In the end, he might've sniffed once or twice as well. During that moment where it wasn't clear whether Julianne might suffer a miscarriage. Then, of course, the Robin Williams antics. They made me sad because his comedic genius was no longer with us. Sure, people died. Some before their time should've run out.

Foster stretched as the credits rolled. "I enjoyed that one as well. You might've made a convert out of me."

I pumped my fist in the air. "Yes, I knew it."

He chuckled. "Okay, let's get you into your coat and on your way. Would you like a slice of cheesecake to take home?"

I gazed at him. "Maybe we can share another night. Or afternoon, or—"

He grasped my cheeks and descended for a hard, fast kiss. I barely had time to register his rough lips before he pulled back. "Yes, Arnav. Yes, to all that."

"Well, I'm grateful you've left me in no doubt." I levered myself so I knelt beside him on the couch. Gently, I took his cheeks in my hands.

He melted into the touch.

I moved closer.

He did the same.

Our lips touched.

Unlike before, this was a gentle kiss. Just a momentary thing. As much as I wanted to deepen it, the time didn't feel right. Tonight's earlier kiss, although agreed to by him, had been what he perceived as an obligation. I needed to make clear to him that he never *owed* me anything. I was here of my own free will.

Hopefully he was as well.

The kiss ended and, regretfully, I rose off the couch. Surprisingly comfortable given its clear age.

I headed toward the front closet.

"What about your movies?" Foster trailed behind me.

"Well, I'm coming back tomorrow. Say, early afternoon? Why don't I bring takeout? Do you have a preference?" I slid my feet into my shoes. "Or I can bring some Indian food. I can, uh, cook some up while I review some documents I have to submit to the court on Monday." I sort of planned to raid Mama's leftovers. Or ask Daddy to whip something up while I tried to learn.

"You can cook and do legal work at the same time?" He laughed. "I can barely make oatmeal without burning it."

I had no doubt he was being facetious.

And I planned on raiding Papi's brunch spread. He always made way too much. Even after I took my share, there'd be enough to feed Foster three times over. I always snuck extra down for snacks during the week, so no one would comment if I did that again. "I'll figure something out. Say one o'clock?"

His eyes brightened. "Yeah, that would be nice."

"And perhaps, over lunch, you can tell me a bit about what you do. You've been rather evasive." I took my coat, which he'd retrieved from the closet. As I put it on, I winced inwardly at having chosen fashion over practicality. The thing wasn't designed for snow. "One more kiss for the road?"

"Yeah." He moved easily into my arms. Again, I didn't get a sense of obligation—just of genuine warmth. *How easy would it be to fall for this guy?* We had all the time in the world, though. Unless he met someone else. Or unless he backed away. Both were always possible but, as our lips touched, neither felt probable.

After a chaste kiss that only had my dick stirring a little, I pulled back. "Tomorrow, we talk, okay?"

"And eat cheesecake." He offered me a boyish grin that I found irresistible. His age wasn't even a factor, as far as I was concerned. Except that it gave him more life experience than me—and I didn't consider that a detraction. In fact, quite the opposite. I liked the idea he'd seen more and done more than me. We could teach each other.

He opened the door.

I went to step out. And came up short. "What the fuck?"

"Oh shit." He eyed the two feet of snow that threatened to fall into the house.

I glanced out. The snow wasn't that high, but the wind had picked up and pushed it against the door, which only had a small awning. I squinted and spotted the snow was almost up to my tires where the wind had blown it as well. The roads were completely covered with about a foot of the white stuff. Now, I was a good Canadian boy. I had some sand and a snow brush. I was also an optimistic Cedar Valley boy who didn't carry a shovel because, like, we never got *that* much snow. My parents lived up the hill, though. One very steep hill.

Foster lived near the bottom of the valley.

So, as well as the issue of getting off his street, I had to contend with the uphill climb.

"You have snow tires, right?" Concern laced his voice.

"Yeah, put them on a couple of weeks ago. I drive all over Cedar Valley, and some of the mountains north of Mission City get snow early. We'd done well this year...or so I'd thought."

Foster nudged the door closed. "Why don't we see what the municipality is saying?" He grabbed his phone from the coffee table and scrolled. "Uh, although snow crews are out, the RCMP is asking everyone to stay off the roads unless it's an emergency. Apparently more snow is on the way." He glanced up to meet my gaze. "I don't...I mean if you really want to go—"

"In that shit? Uh...no." I scratched my cheek. "I can make it to the Grand Hotel. I think."

"That's going downhill."

"Yeah."

"According to the website, the hills are super slippery. Going either way would be dangerous. Where do you live?"

I waved northward, sort of making a gesture of upward as well.

Clearly, he understood. "Well, you'll just have to stay here tonight. Do you...is there someone you need to tell?" He swallowed.

"Foster?"

"Yes."

"I'm not in a relationship with anyone else. I don't have a roommate either." *I should text Mama, but I can do that while you're getting ready for bed. Nothing you need to know about.*

"Okay." Slowly he nodded. "This is kind of obvious, but I'm not either."

"I appreciate your honesty."

He considered in that way that connoted thought—with a furrow in his brow. "But I don't understand why you're not." He rubbed his brow.

I toed off my shoes, then shucked out of my coat and handed it to him. "The reason I'm single is complicated."

"Uh, okay. Why don't you take off your coat, and I'll hang it up. I have a spare pair of pajamas. They'll be short and too wide, but I'm sure we can figure something out."

"Thank you. And well, we've kind of got all night." About our relationship statuses and anything else that might come up. "And tomorrow, if the roads aren't cleared."

"We can wash your clothes if we need to." He held my gaze. "Stay as long as you need to, okay?"

"I can do that."

He let out an exhalation.

I hadn't realized he was holding his breath. Because he was worried about me? Because he was concerned I'd venture out into a near-blizzard? Or because he really wanted me to stay?

I didn't have an answer for that.

Only time would tell.

Chapter Ten

Foster

Staying cool was proving difficult. As I perched on the edge of my bed, waiting for Arnav to finish using the bathroom, I frowned. This house only had one bed. I'd only ever needed one bed. The couch downstairs was too short for me, let alone Arnav, who was several inches taller.

Do I admit the truth or just play along with his casual suggestion we share the bed?

A bed certainly big enough to hold two grown men.

He hadn't suggested we'd do anything sexual.

I shuddered. Not that I minded. Actual *sex* wasn't bad. I hadn't enjoyed anal intercourse much before but, in retrospect, that had been my abysmal choice of partner rather than the act itself.

Or so you tell yourself. Maybe sex with everyone sucks.

Yeah, I didn't entirely buy that. Otherwise, why would people keep doing it? And maybe the guys at work were just bragging about how good they were and how much they loved sex. But their wives regularly got pregnant and had children. No correlation between sexual pleasure and the number of offspring one might produce—but causation was pretty clear.

"Hey, you okay?" Arnav stepped into the room. "You look really deep in thought."

"Just..." I swept my hand across the bed.

He put his neatly folded pile of clothes on my relaxation chair. "Are you worried I might try something?"

I made a point of gazing at myself—with considerable heft and muscles—versus him. All sinew and rangy muscles. Unless he had a black belt I didn't know about, I wasn't really worried. I also wasn't worried because he just didn't come across as that kind of guy. A guy who would take advantage. Who would coerce. Who would force.

But you've been wrong before.

Fucking hell. I tried to silence my inner critic. He could be a bastard sometimes. "No, not that you'll try something." I glanced down.

He advanced to just before me, so I could see his very naked tanned feet. At least I had plush carpeting in this room.

He tucked his finger under my chin and slowly coaxed me into looking up at him.

His luminous dark-brown eyes sparkled in the lamplight. Whether that was just a trick of light or because his actual amusement, I couldn't be certain. Then his expression sobered. "What aren't you telling me?"

I winced. "I, uh, don't usually sleep in a bed."

His eyes widened. "Okay, you're going to have to explain that. You're sitting on a bed."

I nodded.

"It's the only bed in this house—that I saw, anyway?"

I shook my head.

He cocked his head.

Even as I held his gaze, I reached under the bed and tugged.

His eyes widened as he took in the tartan fabric.

"You sleep on a dog bed?"

"Yeah." Slowly, I used my foot to push the bed back under the frame of the adult bed. "I, uh, put it away when people come over. Well, I should clarify that aside from when I had a couple of buddies from work help me with construction, you're the only guy who's actually been here."

"Okay." His brow was still furrowed.

"So, see, we don't have to share the adult bed. You can have it to yourself."

"Foster?"

"Yes?"

"Do you want to sleep on your dog bed tonight? What would you have done if I wasn't here?"

"I sleep on it every night. Well, many nights. I mean, it's the size of a human bed...just in the shape of a dog bed. I like to curl up, and this sounds way too weird. Normal people don't do this."

"I loathe the word *normal*. What's normal anyway? Growing up straight, cis, and boring? Marrying and having two kids? Staying together until one or both of you dies? How many people do you know who actually do that?"

I winced at his sharp tone.

"Sorry. Truly, I apologize. I mean, my parents are in the midst of that. Only seven kids, not two...but you get the gist. And—" He winced again. "—okay, most of my sisters are doing that. I'd hoped at least one would be a lesbian, or even bi, but no such luck. I'm the only queer member of the family. Well, at least the only one who's come out." He waved his hand. "None of that was the point. We are humans with free will. We have to conform to certain societal norms—like not breaking the law. Beyond that, whatever we do in our own homes, as long as we aren't hurting anyone, is fine."

"So, me sleeping like a dog—"

He arched an eyebrow.

Right. Apparently he doesn't want me demeaning myself. "Sleeping in a dog bed," I quickly amended.

His expression softened a bit. "Why don't you show me your bed?"

I tried to judge his thoughts, but that proved challenging. I'd never told anyone else about this. Howard knew, of course. Had threatened to tell people on a couple of occasions. Which should've been a warning sign, but I hadn't taken it as such. In the end, that hadn't mattered anyway. I rose, grasped the edge of the dog bed, and pulled it out. Fortunately, the room was big enough that I had adequate floor space. Because this bed was big enough to hold an adult and a large dog. The two were meant to cuddle. I just had a dog stuffie I cuddled with at night. I wanted a dog of my own...but that was a whole other story.

"Foster, that's a lovely bed." Arnav looked at the blue-and-green tartan fabric over a super comfy bed with a raised edge that kept me snug inside.

Sometimes I needed to stretch, and so I'd flop my legs over the side. Mostly, though, I just cuddled within with my stuffie and a warm comforter.

"Why were you afraid to show me this? Were you worried I'd judge?"

I nodded vigorously.

"Do you want to sleep in your bed tonight?"

I nodded vigorously.

"Then you shall. I always want you to be honest with me, okay? In our relationship, honesty is critical."

"Uh..."

"Yes." He prompted me with both the word and a bob of his head.

"Are we in a *relationship*?" Such a big word. Such massive implications.

"Do you want to be?" He put his hands on his hips, but I had to hold in a laugh. The drawstring was keeping the sleep pants from falling down. They rode low on his hips, and were still a good three inches too short. Who knew ankles could be so sexy?

"I don't know what I want, Arnav." I held his gaze. "I tried a relationship. Once. In forty-five years. It ended disastrously. I don't know where I found the courage to go to Kink three nights ago, but I did. And I met you. I just...don't know what any of this means."

His expression softened, with his eyes losing some of their flint. "How about we discuss this in the morning? Do you have bread, milk, and eggs? Well, you have milk, of course, but the others?"

I nodded.

"Great. I'll make French toast, and you can talk."

Because maybe he thought I'd be more comfortable if he was occupied? *Yeah, good luck with that.*

He grinned. "I can make French toast. I don't cook much. Oh, I could fry up bacon if you have it."

"Bacon?" That didn't seem right, but I wasn't sure how Indians felt about pork.

He shrugged. "Well, my diet is quite Canadian. My mother would prefer I adhere to more rules, but she's also pretty much given up. I mean, I make a mean roti and add a nice curry mix, but something tells me you don't have curry."

"Uh…no." I barely had garlic.

"So, I'll whip up French toast, and you can tell me as little or as much as you want. Now…" He eyed me. "Do you have a bedtime routine? Is there something you need to do?"

I stood very still.

"Foster…" A bit of bite in that tone.

"I get my stuffie and blankie and get into bed."

"And do you want snuggles or petting before bed?"

I didn't answer. I couldn't. Because what he asked might've been simple to him—but it meant everything to me.

"Well, why don't you grab your blankie and stuffie? If you want petting and scritches, you can ask for them, and if I'm way off the mark, then I'll just get into bed, turn off the light, and we'll call an end to a very long day."

After a moment, I scurried over to the closet and retrieved both my down comforter and my stuffie.

"May I see?" Arnav held out his hand.

I didn't read it as a command…more of a request. I placed Chili in his hand.

The black lab was a bit of a chunk, but Arnav handled him easily. He examined my favorite toy. "You really love this."

I nodded.

"You've lovingly repaired him several times." He met my gaze. "Him?"

"Yes. Chili. He's my favorite. I try to take care of him, but he's getting old." I blinked.

Arnav handed him back. "You treasure him and that's great. We all need some source of comfort in our lives. I have my family…although I'm not going to snuggle with them in my bed."

I forced a laugh. Jealousy ripped through me and threatened to bring me to my knees. I wanted that. But had never been privy to it.

"Lie down, Foster. I'll get you tucked in."

I nodded furiously. I got into bed and pulled Chili protectively to my chest.

Arnav pulled the comforter over me and tucked it around me.

I'd likely be too hot at some point and I'd stick a naked foot out but, for the moment, I was incredibly grateful for his kindness.

Slowly, he stroked my head. "You're a good boy, Foster. You know that, right? That you're perfect? That I'm so lucky to know you?"

I wasn't perfect. He would've been more lucky if he'd hooked up with one of the younger pups at Kink the other night.

He narrowed his eyes at me.

After swallowing hard, I uttered, "thank you."

He nodded slowly.

"Uh..." I scrunched my nose. The next words felt critical. That using the right name was so important. Something that showed how much I respected him. How I hoped he might have a place in my life. If only for tonight. I was scared but, in that moment, I acknowledged what I wanted most in the whole wide world. "Daddy?"

A broad grin spread across his face. "Good choice."

For me, that was the only one that felt right. His easy nature and kindness leant itself to me being at ease. Daddy felt...just right.

He pressed a kiss to my forehead. "Goodnight, Foster."

"Goodnight, Daddy."

He rose, headed over to the bed, got under the covers, checked his phone, and smiled. He met my gaze. "My sister sent a funny text. I'll show it to you in the morning. If you wake up and you need something, you just let me know, okay?"

"Yes, Daddy."

"Goodnight, pup."

"Goodnight."

I'd assumed it would take me forever to fall asleep. After all, this was the first night I'd ever had company. But no, with Daddy's breathing clear across the room, I settled into a feeling of contentment and fell right asleep.

Chapter Eleven

Arnav

Awareness came in degrees. A light snore caught my attention first. I smiled to myself.

Foster had settled right away last night—as if a weight had been lifted from his shoulders as I'd made it clear I heartily approved of his dog bed. I didn't mind in the least. Clearly, for him, the bed was a safe space. I had nothing but respect for that.

In the weak late fall light filtering through the curtains, I noted he had a foot stuck out from under the comforter but that the rest of him was burrowed inside. *Ah, his handy temperature-regulation mechanism.* Plain, old-fashioned, and highly effective apparently.

My bladder wasn't happy, and I slid out of bed as quietly as I could and made my way to the bathroom. I pissed, washed my hands, then quickly ran my hand through my hair to make it *just right*. That flop at the top was getting a little long, so I needed to head to see Quelle at the beauty salon. They always did such an amazing job, and although my dad was a fan of the barber in town, I liked a little style to go with my cut. Probably could've gotten that at the barbershop, but I liked getting the gossip too, and Quelle fit the bill perfectly. They, like me, had grown up in Mission City. They knew everyone. *Everyone*. And if they didn't know someone, they knew *of* that someone.

Which made me wonder about Foster. I couldn't remember ever having seen him around town. But then I was always so busy, I often didn't take in the faces around me. Except his handsome features would've had me taking notice, I was certain. Had he grown up in town? No way for me to know. He wasn't of my generation. Which should've scared me, but totally didn't. He was, by my calculation, at the very end of Gen X. Maybe a Millennial, but I questioned that. And I was Gen Z by a few days. He was a Latch Key Kid while I was Gen Next.

Could we meet somewhere in the middle? Because, truly, age was just a number. His kindness and almost...naïveté...spoke to me. Maybe he was experienced in all the ways that counted.

But I didn't get that sense.

He'd hinted he'd had one bad relationship. That broke my heart for someone as sensitive as Foster. I'd had plenty of flings and short-lived affairs—but they'd all gone well and ended amicably enough. I'd been clear going in that I wasn't looking for long-term. In turn, plenty of guys didn't want commitment either. Especially when we'd been in university. Still trying to find our places in the world. Often coming from all around that world to study at a prestigious law school. More often than not, heading out into the world beyond Vancouver or even Cedar Valley as soon as we graduated.

No regrets.

I'd come home where I could do the most good.

Moving back into the family home might've been a miscalculation, though.

Oh well.

I eased the bathroom door open, relieved it didn't creak.

Only to hear rustling from the bedroom.

I made my way over there to find Foster folding up his comforter. He'd already made my bed. When he spotted me, he stilled. "Oh, did you want to get back into bed? I was kind of presumptuous, but I always make the bed. Uh, all the beds."

Making my way over to him, I was careful to telegraph my movements. I grasped his cheeks in my hands and drew him in for a sweet kiss. No tongue. Just a brushing of the lips. "Good morning."

His eyes were a little glassy. "Good morning." He held the comforter against his chest like a shield.

We had a long way to go before he was comfortable with me. "Why don't you have a shower? Or why don't I go first? Then, when you're showering, I can start breakfast." My clothes were barely worn, so putting them back on wasn't a big deal.

"Um. Shouldn't I be cooking for you? You're the guest."

"Didn't we agree last night I'd make French toast?"

"Well...yeah."

"But you thought I didn't mean it?"

"Well...yeah."

"Ah. To be clear, Foster, I say what I mean and mean what I say. So, if I say I want to cook your breakfast, it's because that's what I want. Now, if you object on principle and want to eat cold pizza—"

He winced.

"Right. That's what I hoped you'd say. We can heat up pizza later in the day if I'm still here."

"The road isn't plowed yet. When they do, I think your car's going to be piled high."

Which made me think of my running shoes and light jacket. Wow, I'd truly miscalculated. Something I didn't do often. But when I did, the results were often epic. "Well, I'm certain you have a shovel."

"I do."

"Then I'll borrow it to dig out. Like I said, I have snow tires. So everything will be okay."

"Or..."

"Or...?"

"You could, you know, stay until the snow melts."

He gazed up at me through his lashes.

I laughed. "You're an imp. Do you want me to stay?"

"Truthfully?"

He nodded.

"Uh, yes, I want you to stay. But only as long as you're happy here."

His comment struck me because I honestly believed I could be happy. Here. With him. "Let's play it by ear. We'll see what damage the snowplow does." I moved to the window to peer out. This bedroom faced the backyard.

"Oh, you have to look from the den." He led me across the hallway.

A chill had permeated my feet, and the idea of a hot shower and getting into my clothes held great appeal. Still, I followed him and gazed outside to the winter wonderland with so much snow that the tires on my SUV were almost completely buried. "How much...?"

"I'll check the weather app while you're in the shower."

I waved him off. "Doesn't really matter, does it? Unless you're super curious—"

He pressed a kiss to my cheek. Just a peck. "As long as you don't have somewhere to be, I have no complaints. I like having you here."

He eyed me. "Now, breakfast and then more rom-coms? I'll dig you out once the snowplow's been down the street."

"I can dig myself out."

"Uh, yeah. No. I saw your running shoes. And that jacket's a joke. I won't have you freezing and getting all wet."

Even as he said the words, I noticed a light snow continuing to fall. If I went out in that, I'd get soaked for certain. "Can I make lunch then? Hot chocolate and maybe chili?"

He grinned. "Why do you think I named my dog that? It's one of my favorite foods. Comfort, you know?"

I did know. And it was one of the things I was actually good at making. "Okay. I'm not happy about you doing all the manual labor, but I do like the idea of cooking for you."

"I like that too." Unbidden, he brushed my stubbled jaw. "I do manual labor a lot. I might be the foreman, but I often dig in and help out. That's who I am."

"Maybe I can give you a massage when you're done. Or run you a hot bath."

"You don't have to." His gaze turned wary.

Who hurt you? I want to rip him to shreds with my bare hands. Which wasn't like me. I was about using words to resolve issues. Never brute strength. Except he made me want to use fists instead of affidavits.

"We'll see." He pointed to my feet. "They're turning blue."

He wasn't entirely wrong. Well, the color wasn't actually blue, but they were blocks of ice. "Right. Shower." I allowed him to lead me back to the primary bedroom where I scooped up my neatly folded pile of clothes. By the time I was in the bathroom, he'd retrieved a couple of fluffy towels for me from the linen closet.

"There's a spare toothbrush in the medicine cabinet. Still wrapped. We're going to have to share toothpaste."

I pressed a quick peck to his lips. "I think I'll survive."

He met my gaze with luminous dark-brown ones. "Yeah, I think we will. Normally I'm a shower-at-night guy, but I like the idea of showering while you cook." He winked, and then was gone.

With that in mind, I showered quickly. He had a moisturizing body wash, which I appreciated. I hadn't felt much of his skin—something I intended to rectify today. The two-in-one shampoo was a generic brand, but I was going to be good, so I tucked away the part of me who wanted to buy him the expensive stuff. Meenakshi had once accused me of being a shampoo snob. Likely because she needed the harsh dandruff version, and it didn't do any favors to her hair. No amount of conditioning was going to cover up her disastrous hair. I felt sorry for my older sister—which only made her madder.

I kept my shower short as I didn't know if he had hot water on demand, like we did at our house, or if he had a hot water heater.

Drying myself off took little time with the wonderful-smelling towels. My father was supersensitive to scents—they tended to give him migraines. Everything in our house was as scent-free as we could make them. My rebellious-teenager phase had included some truly wretched cologne. Only took me making my father sick one time for me to throw it out. I opted for soap and water plus deodorant, and what I now understood was that I smelled just fine without the strong additional scents. On the other hand, I didn't do manual labor all day.

I slipped my underwear on and thrust my feet into my socks before they got cold again. I never judged those who worked with their bodies for a living. I didn't even mind the scent of sweat—if it was coming from someone like Foster. The scent of sweat from someone lying to me on the witness stand? Kind of gross. Fear smelled different. And I hoped to never smell it from Foster.

By the time I was fully dressed, the steam from my shower had dissipated. I ran my fingers along my cheeks and decided stubble was a good look for me. Because I wasn't going to use a disposable razor of his as well. I brushed my teeth, belatedly realizing maple syrup and mint weren't going to mix well and then deciding fresh breath was more important as I intended to kiss Foster.

If he let me.

I found him sitting in a bathrobe, perched on the side of his bed, typing something into his phone. He kept squinting.

"Foster?"

"Hmm?"

"Do you need glasses?"

He winced. "Sorry."

I blinked. "For what?"

"I, uh, yeah. I do need glasses. I have some, in fact, reading glasses."

"And you're not wearing them because...?"

"I look dorky."

That line could've been a question or a statement. I took it as a statement. "Where are they?"

He pointed to his nightstand.

I retrieved the glasses, carefully tucked in a case. I unfolded them and then, very carefully, put them on his face.

He winced.

I grinned. "That's, like, so fucking sexy."

He narrowed his eyes.

"You ever look at yourself in the mirror? Say whatever you want, but those frames are perfect for you. I think you should wear glasses all the time."

He pulled them off. "Yeah, well, that's never going to happen." He rose, put them back in their case, and closed the nightstand drawer. "I'm going to have a shower." He strode from the room. Leaving his phone on the bed—open and waiting for someone to snoop.

Well, I wasn't that person. Tempted? Of course. Willing to cross that line? Oh hell, no.

So I texted Mama and then headed downstairs to make breakfast.

Chapter Twelve

Foster

The scent of bacon wafted upstairs to me as I put my jeans and a clean shirt on.

You're going to have to tell him everything. Then he can leave, and you'll be alone, but you'll have done the right thing.

Tears pricked my eyes at the idea.

Arnav hadn't ridiculed my dog bed. He'd tucked me in and kissed me goodnight.

I didn't *always* sleep in the dog bed. But when I'd had a stressful day—or was just feeling lonely—I made that choice. Yesterday had been the opposite of lonely. Pizza and three movies? Holding him as he'd cried? Sharing some tenderness? Those weren't things that people did alone.

Well, duh.

I stuffed my feet into my slippers and headed downstairs. My friend preferred laminate flooring in the house, which was fine, but I tended to run the house a little cool to save on heating costs which meant the floors were pretty much always cold. Great in the summer—crappy in the middle of a cold, wet autumn.

Arnav greeted me with a huge smile and a plate of bacon. "I made myself at home. I figured if you had it, then you wouldn't mind."

"I don't mind. I don't eat it often." I rolled my eyes. "Have to watch my health."

"That's right. Because I want you around for a long time." He pressed a kiss to my lips—completely catching me off guard—then handed me the plate.

I managed a smile.

"What?" He cocked his head.

"Just..." I swallowed. "When I tell you about my past, then you're going to take off."

He frowned. "Foster." Said with part exasperation and part admonishment.

"Yeah?"

"Did you break the law?"

"No."

"Did you intentionally hurt someone?"

"Well, no." *Definitely not.*

"So why are you convinced I'm going to take off? Do you not believe I can be fair?" His expression softened. "Do you not trust me?"

Big question with huge ramifications. But an honest one. "I do trust you. Maybe it's myself I don't trust."

"God, I'm so sorry. I want to hug you, but I need your permission, and I don't want to burn the French toast."

"Yeah, burning would be bad." I eyed the bacon, nestled in some paper towels to absorb the fat. "How about I set the table?"

"That would be perfect." He snagged me around the waist and pressed a quick kiss to my temple. "Good morning, pup."

I beamed. "Good morning...uh, Daddy."

He turned back to the griddle and flipped the toast, showing a nice browning. "Do you mind calling me Daddy? Is there another word you prefer?"

I placed the plate on the table and set about collecting cutlery, glasses, plates, and orange juice from the fridge. I hardly ever drank it, but sometimes I enjoyed the tart taste. "Um." I considered. "I don't really like handler—too impersonal. Now, if I was referring to you as something when speaking to someone else, then maybe? And alpha connotes a relationship I don't think we have. You're not a pack mate."

"Alpha can have other meanings."

After putting the silverware in the proper place, I met his gaze. "I prefer Daddy." I winced. "That's not what I called...*him*. So having something special between the two of us feels like the right thing to do."

Arnav placed two plates of French toast on the table. He'd already put out the butter and syrup. I didn't usually add butter—not good for my cholesterol—but I hoped he'd indulge in whatever made him happy. He returned to grab the coffee he'd made himself from the machine. It pleased me that he'd made himself at home.

We both sat.

I passed him the plate of bacon. He grabbed a couple of slices, and then gestured for me to have some as well. I rarely did, and he'd raided my freezer to find it, but again, I was pleased he'd felt comfortable doing that. I wanted him to feel like he could do anything here. After he dug into his food, I did as well.

The French toast tasted divine with just a touch of added syrup.

He'd drowned his, which I found amusing.

I took another bite. "Is this cinnamon?"

"Yes." He picked up his coffee. "I like the added flavor. Is it to your liking?" He sipped.

"Oh yes. This is..." I swallowed. "No one's done this for me in a very long time."

He arched an eyebrow. "Well, that's going to change. I'm not a great chef, but I'm willing to learn. At the very least, we can prepare some meals together."

My little kitchen would ensure we were close together as we prepared food. "I like that idea." I eyed him shyly. "So you'll come back?"

"I would like to. But only if you're willing. I'm not going to force you into a relationship. Into more than you think you can handle. More than you want."

Don't show too much enthusiasm. "I think I'd like a relationship with you." I slid a bite of French toast through the syrup, but didn't eat. "I appreciate that you let me be myself last night."

Unexpectedly, he grasped my hand. Unexpectedly—but not unwelcome.

"You can always be yourself with me. Whatever makes you comfortable. I want you to enjoy your life, Foster. If that means sleeping in a dog bed and playing on the ground, I'm fine with that. If that means going to Kink on pup night and throwing yourself into the pile while I sit back with the other handlers and watch? Well, I'm okay with that as well. Your eyes lit up when I gave you scritches last night—don't think I didn't see that. I want to be the one to bring you joy. If that means letting you explore and grasp your nature, I'm fine with that. Everyone has a different path. Yours is to be a pup. Mine is to be a Daddy. Hopefully your Daddy."

"We've known each other four days." I whispered the words.

"True. And I'm sure Master Dante and Evan would be the first to caution you. Have you spoken to either of them?"

I shook my head.

"Well, I think you should. Dante can vouch for me—at least as far as he's vetted me. And Evan can offer you support if you need it. He can connect you with other pups. I'm encouraging you to reach out and, if possible, find friends. I don't ever want you to be isolated."

"He did that to me." I put my fork down.

"Ah." Arnav squeezed my hand. "Perhaps we can eat now and then talk after breakfast? I'd like to hear about the relationship—if you're comfortable talking about it. I want to know what your triggers are. Because it's legitimate that there are things I might do that will upset you. You trusted someone, and they betrayed that trust. That hurts."

I blinked several times, then met his gaze. "Have you ever...?"

He shook his head. "I'm going to be honest with you—I've only had a few relationships, and they were well-defined and of limited durations. You make me think more might be possible. And I suppose I should examine those feelings carefully. Except I know you're the one I want. The right person for me. I'm hoping, in time, that we'll find a way to forge some kind of relationship." With the hand not holding mine, he snagged his coffee cup. "And I hope, in time, you'll come to trust me." He sipped.

But I do trust you. I'm not sure I should...but I do. Aloud, I said, "That would be nice."

"Can you finish your breakfast?"

I did a literal gut check. Not wanting my old...boyfriend...to dictate whether or not I was comfortable eating the rest of the delicious meal Arnav had made. "I'm okay. Yes, I can finish."

He squeezed my hand one more time, then let it go.

I missed the contact, but also understood we each needed two hands to eat.

We consumed the rest of the meal in a companionable silence. Not fraught or anything like that. Just quiet and comfortable. When we were both clearly finished, I offered a smile. "May I clear the dishes and make you another cup of coffee?"

Arnav grinned. "That would be lovely. Perhaps I'll look outside to see if the road has been plowed. I'll also need to check my messages."

"Of course." Except I hoped the street wasn't plowed. Because then he'd have to stay. Well, if I dug out my pickup truck, I could certainly drive him wherever he needed to go. *I might not mention that option right away. He said I could talk about my relationship with Howard. If I don't do it right now, I might chicken out.* Offhand, I couldn't think of any triggers, but that didn't mean I didn't have any. Well, aside from the obvious one—I didn't want to be ridiculed or put down. About anything. Ever. If I made a mistake, I was happy to have it pointed out to me so I could learn. But ridicule hurt in a way I wasn't even certain I could articulate.

Despite my protestation, Arnav took his empty plate and glass into the kitchen. He still had a few sips left of his coffee, so he took the mug with him into the living room. He'd only used the number of dishes absolutely necessary, so cleaning up took little time. I turned on the dishwasher and made him a fresh cup of coffee in a new mug. I was just about to take it to him when he appeared.

"So, no plowing yet, but the city website says soon. Good thing I don't live in the hills north of Mission City. The plows aren't likely to get there until later in the afternoon at the earliest."

"Where do you live?"

His eyes widened.

Shit, was I not supposed to ask that question?

He cleared his throat. "On a cul-de-sac near the Abbey."

Okay, not very helpful. Everything from two-bedroom bungalows to mansions were within a mile radius of Westminster Abbey. The old building was atop the highest hill in Mission City proper. I'd gone up once to see the view which spanned much of Cedar Valley and the mighty Fraser River. Well over to Abbotsford and even a view of Mount Baker, the dormant volcano in Washington State. So, that he lived near the Abbey told me little.

None of my business. Just because I'm curious, doesn't mean I'm entitled to the information. "That sounds nice. I hope to one day get a place of my own. Not that I don't love this place..." I gazed around the small space. Cozy enough for one. Okay for two, I supposed. Except a bit on the cramped side. Once the downstairs renovations were completed, there'd be more space.

"This is a lovely home. If you wanted to buy, could you get a mortgage?"

"I can't afford this place on my salary, and my savings aren't enough. I'll keep trying, but I likely won't have enough of a down payment for a condo until I'm fifty. And that means working until I'm seventy-five just to pay the damn mortgage off. That all feels overwhelming. So maybe I'm just meant to rent for the rest of my life. Nothing wrong with that."

Arnav moved to my side. "Of course not."

"He wouldn't let me work." I blinked. "I had to stay at home and serve him. And then he'd make fun of me and put me down because I wasn't contributing."

"Christ. What an asshole."

I couldn't even muster up a smile. I cleared my throat. "Can we sit?"

"Of course." He gestured to the couch.

I sat on one end.

He sat on the other end, but very close to the middle. He put one arm on the back, reaching out toward me. In his other hand, he held his coffee. "Okay, so share what you want. Don't feel you have to say anything or not say anything that you think might hurt me. I'm a big boy. Honesty is critical."

"Yeah, okay."

Chapter Thirteen

Arnav

Let him come to you. Don't push. Yet pushing was exactly what I wanted to do. In my professional life, I knew when to come on strong and when to use the slow-and-gentle approach. This situation called for the latter, but all I wanted to do was the former. *Like a bull in a china shop—you might ruin everything before you get what you want.* So I sipped my coffee and waited for Foster to share what he could. Of course, I'd already decided to find out as much as I could about this ex of his. To make sure he wasn't mistreating anyone else.

Or so I told myself.

Foster clasped his hands on his lap. After a long moment of staring at them, he turned his attention to the beautiful, large, plate-glass window with the curtains now pulled back, unlike last night.

The snow had lessened from the blizzard and now fell lazily. The winds had died as well, so the flakes descended in a more orderly pattern. If snow could even ever be called *orderly*.

"I don't think he was a bad man."

I refocused my attention on Foster, even though he didn't look at me.

He drew in yet another deep breath, then blew it out slowly. "Just...controlling. Which you'd think would be a good trait in a Dominant."

I held in my snort. But just barely. There were some very unhealthy ways for a Dom to be controlling.

"And slowly I became more isolated. Much like I had been as a kid. He knew that too. I'd stupidly told him all about my upbringing. The bad stuff. He'd use that against me."

I wanted to know in what way—and about his childhood in general—but his last Dom had used those secrets against him. If I wanted his trust, I needed to make sure I let him keep his privacy as long as he needed to. Instead, I waited for him to come to me.

"And...I don't know...I didn't argue. Well, not after the first bit. Defiance was met with swift punishment. Not always physical. No, he was more into psychological stuff. Deprivation, cruelty, callousness. Anything he could do to hurt me and to break me down."

Again, holding in my anger took effort.

"Then one day he told me he was finished with me. That I could move out. That he'd found someone younger. Someone more attractive."

"Okay, sorry, I have to say something. That's utter bullshit. Don't get me wrong—I'm glad you're away from that fucker, and I hope you never see him again, and he better hope I never see him because being an abusive fucking asshole is totally unacceptable."

Finally, he turned to meet my gaze. His eyes were shiny with unshed tears.

"Do you..." I hesitated, not knowing the right thing to say. The right thing to do.

"Can I have a hug?"

I barely had a chance to nod before he lunged for me. I caught him against my chest and managed to put the empty mug on the coffee table before pulling him fully into my arms.

He shook. *Is he crying? Yep, that's wetness.* I didn't care, of course. I only hoped these were cathartic tears. That if something inside him had broken, I'd be able to help him put it back together.

As he clung to me, I held him close while rubbing his back. He'd hinted at physical punishments as well as clear psychological abuse. I'd sort of guessed at some of that. His reactions. His little comments. His wariness around me. Yet he was also comfortable around Dante, who was the consummate Dom so, to me, that offered a glimmer of hope. That he might come to trust I would never—never—do anything to betray his faith in me.

"I'm sorry." He sniffed and pulled back.

Reluctantly, I let him. I wasn't going to hold him against his will. "For what?"

"For being a crybaby."

"Okay, that's just bullshit. I don't know if *he* said something to you or if some asshole kid on the schoolyard used that term—"

"A worker in a group home." He whispered the words.

Oh shit. This was turning out to be so much worse than I'd imagined. "Do you want to talk about it? How long were you in the group home?"

He sniffed.

I spotted a box of tissue. I snagged it and offered it to him.

His watery smile was somewhat reassuring. He grabbed a couple of tissues and wiped at his nose.

"You can blow your nose, if you need to."

He blinked.

"It's all right. Perfectly normal. I do it frequently myself. Seasonal allergies."

"In front of other people?"

"Well...maybe not before a judge or opposing counsel. But in front of my family? We're all human."

The smile widened. "I think I like the sound of your family."

"Yes, well, they keep me on my toes." *And I'm not going to mention I still live with them*.

He blew his nose, then tucked the tissue into his pocket. "I'm okay."

I questioned that, but wouldn't say anything out loud. "Can you...do you want to talk about what happened? Before?"

"You mean when I was growing up?" He blinked.

"Yes. I mean, you've already said a lot, and maybe it's overwhelming...or maybe it's better to just say everything all at once and get it over with."

"This is a lot of burdening."

I cocked my head.

"Me burdening you." He gestured between the two of us.

"Ah." I offered a measured smile. Just so he wouldn't think I was enjoying this or getting some perverse pleasure out of his clear pain. "If you're unburdening yourself, there's nothing wrong with that. I'm here to listen. I'm not a therapist, but I'm still good at hearing what you are and aren't saying."

He let out a little huff of a laugh. Then he rubbed his face. "My mom...had issues. My dad took off when I was little. I don't remember him. My mom had a...I want to say some kind of breakdown. When I was eight. I was sent to live in a group home while she recovered. Only she didn't. Well, not for a long time."

"That had to be rough."

"Yeah, well..." He swallowed. "I was a scrawny kid. Always picked on. Always made fun of. I mean, those other kids didn't have parents either, but somehow they were fine with it."

"Or so they appeared to be."

He nodded. "Yeah, I figured that out as an adult. Their way of coping with the pain was to harass the new kid. Some kids came after me, but I tried to stand up to them. Wound up getting my ass kicked a time or two. But I kept at it. Then, when I was twelve, I moved into a foster home." He rubbed his face again. "That was like night and day. Suddenly I was living with a family. Mrs. Stubbs and Papa J. Oh, he was Mr. Stubbs, but he insisted we call him PJ. Short for Papa John. He was..." Foster sniffed. "Like, the best. And there were all these rules about not touching kids and stuff. But if you needed a hug, you could always ask for one from PJ and he never turned you down. Big guy. Like Santa Claus big. And he just smiled all the time. Mrs. Stubbs worked for a doctor's office, and PJ stayed home with the kids. That was unusual back then. Remember, more than thirty years ago now. Things were starting to change, but men didn't generally stay home with the kids. PJ did.

"I went to school and then raced home every day. He would be so proud when I showed him my work. My grades improved. I slept through the night. I made friends. And when the kids made fun of my name—what with Foster being the foster kid—he'd stand up for me. Said I had a great name. Because to foster meant to love. To nurture. And he said one day he could see me doing just that." He sniffed again.

"He sounds like a remarkable man."

"He was." Foster rubbed his face yet again. "I went to his funeral. About...I want to say about fifteen years ago. I hadn't kept in touch, but I saw his obituary in the paper. They talked about the hundred or so kids who'd taken refuge in his home. Whom he'd loved. I just...had to be there. Mrs. Stubbs didn't recognize me. I didn't expect her to, what with having fostered so many. I expressed my love for PJ and then moved along. Not long after that, I met Howard."

"So you were with PJ until you finished high school."

"Uh, no." He laughed bitterly. "My mother got her act together and decided she wanted to get me back. No one asked me what I wanted—which was to stay with PJ. I barely knew my mother, and what I remembered was her being unstable. Anyway, I was sent back to her. She worked, and I went to school, and we barely interacted. No joyous reactions when I did well. No congratulations when I graduated with honors and got a scholarship to the British Columbia Institute of Technology."

I wanted to grab him into an even bigger hug. Sometimes the system really didn't know what was best for the child.

He huffed. "Except she gave me a home, and me leaving PJ's meant he could take in another kid in need."

"That's a very mature response."

"Telling myself that was the only way to work through the pain. And I did. When I graduated high school, my mom suggested I move out. I did. And I never saw her again."

I tried to discern how he felt about that, but I couldn't get a read on him.

"Then, like six years ago, the police notified me that she'd died. She never married and never had kids. Just left a note about me."

"Did she..." I swallowed.

"What? Oh no, nothing like that." He waved me off. "She had a heart condition and knew she was going to go sooner rather than later. She had a nurse who checked in with her three times a week. One day...she was dead." He let out a sigh. "I would've gone to her...if she'd asked. I thought maybe one day...but she never did. And by then I was in the relationship with Howard, and..." He sighed. "I had to ask Howard for the money to cremate her. I think he wanted to just leave her for the government to take care of, but he agreed."

Jesus, I'm going to fucking kill Howard.

"She had almost no stuff. I found a few old photos and kept them. The rest I donated. In the end, she barely made a blip in my life."

"You had PJ. At least for that brief time." Was this the right thing to say? I just didn't know.

"Yeah." He finally met my gaze with glassy eyes. "I wanted to keep in touch after I left his care, but the social worker said I wasn't allowed. I was a rule follower, even back then." He closed his eyes briefly. "I went by his house when I got the scholarship. I mean, I was eighteen and so wasn't having to abide by the rules. He was on the sidewalk, teaching a young girl to ride a bicycle. She looked so happy that I couldn't..." He scrubbed his eyes. "I didn't want to get in the way of that. He'd moved on. He was taking care of someone else. I just thanked God—or whoever—that I'd had him in my life. That he'd been such a positive influence."

"I bet he would've been proud, but you should also be proud of yourself for putting another child first. Then college?"

"Yeah. I studied construction operations. I wanted to be involved in building housing. That seemed like a good use of my skills. And I had some muscle, so I could do a lot of the physical stuff."

"That's can be tough on your body though."

He waved me off. "I was young. And ambitious. Even when construction was in a downturn, I always found work. And, by accident, I found Howard."

And here we circled back. "How, exactly?"

"He was the lead architect on a housing complex. This was for-profit housing, which wasn't my favorite to work on, but the government wasn't in the business of building homes at that point, and I needed the job."

"Just like that?"

He indicated a *so-so* motion with his hand. "We didn't hit it off at first. I found him arrogant, he found me abrasive. But I was only abrasive with him. Something about him just got to me, and so I was always reacting. Then one night, after everyone else had gone home, we had it out. To clear the air." He laughed. A grating sound. "After shouting at each other for about twenty minutes, we…" He clapped his hands together. "We realized we batted for the same team. We realized we were…compatible." He arched an eyebrow.

I knew what he meant, and so nodded.

"He drove us to the nearest motel, and we…discovered how compatible we really were." He shrugged. "I gave up my apartment and moved into his house a month later. Two months after that, I tendered my resignation at work. And then became his fuck toy for about ten years."

My breath caught. I hadn't realized he'd been in that dysfunctional relationship for so long.

"Then he dumped me, and I tried to find a job in Vancouver. Except I couldn't afford to rent in the city and I had no savings and no car." He rolled his eyes. "Yeah, what was I thinking, right? Apparently nothing intelligent."

"And he ended the relationship, you said?"

"Yep, told me to get out. That he'd found someone...livelier." He held my gaze. "Meaning twenty years younger than me."

"Shit."

"Precisely. Howard is a big bear of a man. Attractive to boot. He'd have no problem attracting the twinks. And he found one to his liking. I was simply an inconvenience. And I didn't have a leg to stand on. I hadn't been filing my taxes, so I hadn't told the government we were common law. At that point, it felt a little pointless. I got my taxes filed—having to explain to them how I'd had no income for ten years and wasn't just not reporting it—and then picking up the pieces. I found a construction company in Mission City that was hiring. The foreman saw potential in me. Or so he claimed. Once I'd been working for him for six months, he sent me back to BCIT for my construction-supervisor certificate. My skills were rusty, but not that much had changed. With my new credentials, the foreman put me in touch with a friend of his who needed help. For all of my"—he waved his hand around—"piss-poor judgment in men...I was good at helping people build stuff. Been doing that ever since."

"Here in Mission City?" I was certain I didn't remember spotting him.

"Well, for those first few months. The job he helped me get was over in Abbotsford. I lived in a rental over there." He gestured around. "This is his house. Well, his rental house. We were sharing a beer when he told me about the mess his former tenants left. I offered to help him out—for free. I still owed him big time. He wouldn't accept the help, but he offered me a huge discount on the rent. Like a quarter of what I was paying for a crap-hole apartment in Abby. I moved the next week and have been slowly fixing this place up. He buys all the supplies and stuff. I just provide the labor."

"Sounds like he's getting the better end of the deal." Free labor? Foster should've been getting free rent.

He shook his head. "That place in Abby had black mold. No, I needed out, and there's not much rental supply in the area. I had just landed a new construction project in Mission City. This is perfect. I don't have to drive back and forth over the bridge every day. And I'm working for a not-for-profit. I may be making a bit less money than if I were working for a for-profit developer, but..." He shut his left eye, as if in contemplation.

"You feel better about yourself?"

"Yeah, that."

"It sounds like you've made a good life for yourself."

"Except..." He swallowed, looked down at his hands, then finally looked up to meet my gaze. "I'm lonely."

That, I understood. "Which is why you went to Kink."

"Which is why I went upstairs with you in Quinton's house."

Right. Somehow I had trouble reconciling that man with the one before me. Perhaps because at Quinton's, Foster had seemed full of bravado and confidence. At least until he ran. I'd had no idea about the complex man underneath.

"What do you want, Foster? Right now. What would make you happy?"

He held my gaze. "For you to be with me. In my bed." He waved his hand, as if swatting away a fly. "Not the dog bed. The real bed."

"Okay." *Is this the right thing to do? He just unburdened himself. Am I taking advantage? Is it taking advantage if he's the one doing the asking? Doing the offering?* I eyed him. "How would this work?"

He scratched the back of his neck. "Well, I've got lube and condoms. So yeah, if you wanted that. Or I can just give you a blow job—if you wanted that."

Is he making an assumption about me? "Uh-huh."

"What? Am I getting something wrong?"

"Well..." I cleared my throat. "It's just..." Heat crept into my cheeks.

He laughed. "That's not how you see this going?"

"It's not that. Just...most people see me as a Dominant and assume I also prefer topping. I can top, but I prefer bottoming."

"I get it. Howard was a bear, but he didn't have any interest in topping. That's why we were, uh..."

"Compatible?"

"Yeah."

"Let this be the last time we speak about Howard and his sexual preferences. Unless you feel like sharing, of course." Because dictating who he could or couldn't talk about was way too controlling, and he'd had enough of that for a lifetime.

Foster scooted closer. "I'm good if I close that door forever."

Forever's a long time. Ten years was a long time. Still, for today, I was completely fine with locking Howard away behind mental doors. "So you're in the mood?" I wasn't certain I was, but giving this a try worked for me. I was attracted to Foster. Making him feel good would be a priority. And, hell, if we weren't compatible in all the ways that mattered, then finding out now and maybe moving away from a romantic relationship and into something platonic might be in order. Regardless of how things turned out, I wanted to be his friend.

And I hoped he felt the same way about me.

Chapter Fourteen

Foster

Part of me questioned my sanity as I rose and held my hand out to Arnav. Questioned the wisdom of inviting a man I'd only known for four days to my bed. Loneliness alone didn't explain my bold move. Neither did horniness. After I just word vomited my life before him, I hardly felt like *getting it on*.

So why was I doing this? What did I hope to gain from it?

Tenderness.

I wanted him to hold me. To be gentle with me. And sure, I could've just asked for a snuggle. His hugs weren't fatherly in the same way as PJ's, but they felt damn nice. Even though Arnav wasn't the type of guy I usually was attracted to. I liked men who were big and burly, but he had hidden strength in his slender body that I thought I could count on.

Arnav gasped my hand and rose.

I dithered, suddenly unsure. "Do you need to check the street? I suppose we would've heard the plow." Except I'd been so far gone into the past, I wasn't convinced I would have.

"Unless you're in a rush to kick me out, I don't care if the snowplow has come or not."

"Don't you have someone to get home to?"

He cocked his head.

"You had someone you had to text last night."

His face relaxed with the frown line easing. "There's no one expecting me."

Which wasn't the same as saying he didn't have anyone to go home to, but I'd take his comment at face value. He'd said he wasn't in a relationship. If he was, though, then why had he gone to Kink? Hooked up with me at Quinton's? Unless he had a partner who didn't have the same proclivities... *You're being paranoid. You need to trust him. Trust yourself. Believe that—*

"Stop."

I frowned. I hadn't actually been moving.

"Whatever you're thinking, you can just stop." Arnav moved closer, pressing a thumb to the spot between my eyebrows. "There isn't anyone else. I'm not built like that—and neither are you, I suspect."

"I'm not." Here I could quickly reassure. "I was faithful to—"

He moved his finger to my lips. "I believe you. Would have known it even if you hadn't said anything. I'm just glad you decided to take a one-night stand chance on me at Quinton's. I imagine that's not like you either."

I kissed his finger.

He moved it away.

I grinned. "Okay, like easiest answer ever. You were fucking hot. Like, sinfully hot. And I figured I wasn't likely to get the chance to get lucky again anytime soon. I still hadn't found the courage to go to Kink, and if I dated someone, then explaining about...you know..."

He nodded.

"Right. So a hookup felt...safe."

"And yet might not have been."

I considered. "True. But I wasn't doing anything without a condom, I have a good thirty pounds on you and, no offense, way more muscle—"

"No offense taken, I assure you." He grinned.

"And like thirty people below. Any one of whom would likely come running to my rescue."

"Not that you would've needed it."

"From you? No. I guess I just sensed you were a good person. And hell, I'd missed sex. It'd been a fucking long time and here was this hot guy just offering it. And yeah, I figured why not?"

"But then you ran." His dark-brown eyes pierced my soul.

"Because I panicked."

"Because you panicked." He repeated the words, as if testing them out. Seeing how they fit into the narrative he'd created for us.

"Not just because I worried Quinton might find us—although that was in my mind—but because I enjoyed myself and..." I swallowed. "I almost didn't remember what that was like. To be with someone without the weight of expectations. To just be in the moment and not worry about anything."

"I wish you'd stayed." He caressed my cheek.

"But if I had, I probably wouldn't have had the courage to tell you about my...desires."

He frowned. "I'd like to think that, in time, you would've found the courage."

I shook my head. "I found the courage with—"

Arnav winced.

"—the other guy."

His expression lightened as he chuckled.

I didn't get the feeling he didn't want me to mention *Howard* because he was jealous or anything. More he saw the pain I endured when I brought up the past. "It didn't end well." Hadn't begun all that well either. Once I'd told my ex about my desire to be a pup sometimes, something clearly shifted in our relationship. He'd humored me, but clearly had lost all respect. Not that he'd had much to begin with. Despite the fact he was a big guy, I was the *muscle* in the relationship while he was the *brains.* Never mind that I'd been to college or had been working for ten years. None of that meant anything to him. He liked being fucked while also dominating. He wasn't even a bossy bottom—he was a Top who liked taking it up the ass. To him—and to me—no contradiction existed.

We'd fit until we hadn't.

"I think..." Arnav continued to stroke my cheek. "Have you ever talked to someone about this?"

"I'm talking to you." He seemed like a swift guy, but his question had me hesitating.

"No." His nose twitched.

Is he going to sneeze? Is he allergic to something in my house? He said seasonal allergies, but what it there's something here that's making him sneeze.

Yet he didn't sneeze. "I meant a counselor. Someone who can help you work through some of this."

"I'm fine." I might've snapped that.

He held my gaze. "Maybe that's true. But you've had a lot happen to you—"

"That was years ago." *Please don't bring up the fact I was crying, like, five minutes ago.*

After a long moment, he sighed. "Maybe this wasn't the best time to bring it up."

I squinted. "There's a good time to say to someone that they need to see a therapist?"

He chuckled. "Okay, fair point. We were headed in one direction, and I derailed us."

"Because the idea was on your mind."

"Because the idea was on my mind." Again, he caressed my cheek.

No matter how annoyed with him I might think I was—and knowing I wasn't—I couldn't stay annoyed when he petted me. "A therapist?"

"I can refer you to someone up at Healing Horses Ranch." Before I could speak, he continued. "They offer equine and canine therapy."

My ears perked. "Dogs?"

He smiled. "They have two dogs. One is an official therapy dog, and the other is just…a companion. I have a client who is a therapist up there. Or there are several others." He held up his hand. "I'm not saying you need serious psychological counseling. Well, maybe you do. Who am I to judge? I just think a session or two talking to someone might help. I know if I was ever struggling, I'd go."

"You don't seem like the type who's ever struggled."

"I've been lucky. Someone can put on a good front and, to the outside, they look like they've got their shit together. Meanwhile, on the inside, they're stressed."

He had a point. About people putting on a good front. "One of my guys needed help. I watched him getting worse and worse, and I finally had a talk with him. His kid had been diagnosed with cancer, and he couldn't afford to miss work because the family needed the income and he needed his private insurance. I convinced him to talk to the counselor. You're right—it made a difference." I scratched my chin. I liked to be clean-shaven, but I hadn't bothered this morning. In too much of a hurry and not wanting to miss out on a single moment with Arnav. "Okay, I'll think about it."

He took my cheeks in his hands and placed a gentle kiss to my lips.

I wanted to resent the kiss. Like he was rewarding me for agreeing to something I should've been open to anyway. Except when he pressed his lips to mine again, he applied way more pressure, and heat built inside me. And so I opened to him. I let him lead the kiss, sinking into the pleasure as he devoured me.

He thrust his tongue into my mouth and demanded surrender. He plundered. He insisted. He commanded and showed no mercy as he pressed himself against me.

Thoughts of therapists and dog counselors and horses fled as I surrendered to the wonderful feeling strumming through my veins. Need. Desire. Only today, I wasn't offering myself up as an obligation. I didn't feel like I *had* to give in. I gave in because I wanted to.

He was the first to pull back, his labored coffee-scented breath against my cheek. "As much as I want to say *fuck it, the couch is good enough*, I want to treat you properly. To me, that means showing you reverence in a proper bed."

Reverence. That word meant something. It meant he treasured me. He considered me worthy of something good in life. I was more than just a quick fuck on the closest surface.

And that meant everything.

I offered my hand.

He accepted.

I guided him back up the narrow, creaky staircase to my bedroom. I'd opened the curtains, so the winter light filled the room. To me, snow dampened things. It dampened noise. It dampened light. It dampened pain. Pain I wasn't willing to examine too closely at the moment.

Again, he pulled me into his arms. "This is more like it." He pressed his lips to mine.

On instinct, I opened for him. This time, he pulled me flush against him, letting me feel his erection against my hip.

Okay, that's more like it. The rest of the world could just fuck off as far as I was concerned. And I was incredibly grateful I'd driven over to Abbotsford on Friday night, after we'd decided he would come here last night. To pick up supplies. I hadn't actually believed I'd need them—but I also wasn't going to be caught without them. I could've gone to a pharmacy in Mission City, but I still wanted anonymity. Who knew at forty-five I'd be embarrassed to be seen buying condoms? Lube, I kept a supply of.

"Foster?"

"Yeah?"

Arnav pulled back. "What are you thinking?"

"That I'm glad I bought condoms on Friday night?"

He laughed. "And here I was, worried you were having second thoughts."

I angled my body so my erection brushed his. "We're going to finish what we started on Halloween."

"Oh, I like the sound of that." He snagged the hem of my henley. "You mind?"

In response, I raised my arms.

He yanked the shirt over my head.

I patted my head, as if to push down the hair that was no longer there.

He grinned. And indicated I reciprocate with his shirt.

Which I happily obliged.

His nipples pebbled in the cold air.

"Do you want me to turn up the heat?"

"No way. We're going to be generating plenty of our own shortly."

"I like the sound of that." I caught the waist of his pants and undid the button.

Our gazes met.

He nodded.

I unbuttoned it, then lowered the zipper. I kept right on going, pulling his pants down.

Obligingly, he stepped out of them.

I lowered myself to my knees. When faced with his crotch, I grasped his boxer briefs and gently tugged them down, mindful of his straining erection. His cock sprang free, and I grasped the base. Much as I had a month ago, I angled myself to take him in my mouth.

He moaned.

I licked around the crown, slowly pulling him farther into my mouth. He tasted heavenly—his scent achingly familiar. I'd thought about him every night in the past month and the reality was so much better than the memory. I hollowed my cheeks and sucked as hard as I could. I tongued his slit. I raked my teeth gently down his length. I reveled when his breathing hitched.

Keeping up the steady rhythm, I grasped his balls in my hands. This was something I enjoyed, and I figured I'd try it on him.

He surged, flexing his pelvis and thrusting his cock farther down my throat.

I nearly gagged. Undaunted, I pulled back far enough to continue my assault. *I want to make this good for you—*

"I'm going to come."

Well, good. I sucked harder.

He came.

With pleasure, I swallowed. He tasted good and, just as importantly, I wanted him to see how much I treasured this. I gazed up.

He pressed a hand to my cheek, even as he swayed.

I popped off and offered him a sheepish smile.

"I hadn't forgotten how fucking good you are at that."

My heart soared. Arnav wasn't someone who said something he didn't mean. He spoke candidly. He might sometimes couch things in softer language, but he was a straight shooter.

"You're going to fuck me now...right?" His dark-brown eyes glinted with humor.

"Oh, definitely."

I took the hand he offered and let him pull me up. And I ignored the shot of pain through my left knee.

He met my gaze. Then he lowered his hands to the button of my jeans.

I nodded.

He reciprocated by unbuttoning them and lowering the zipper. Then he snagged the waistband of my jeans and my briefs and pulled them both down at the same time, dropping to one knee so he could guide my feet.

I rested my hand on his shoulder as I stepped out of my clothes. Where I expected him to stand, though, he kept kneeling and grasped the base of my shaft. He gave me no chance to think as he sucked me into his mouth. *Oh holy fuck.* The unexpected wet warmth around my cock rocketed a full body shiver through me. This was a nearly new sensation. Howard had never gone down on me. Not once in ten years. A few guys in fumbling encounters in my twenties—but none worth remembering.

No way was I ever going to forget Arnav. His talented tongue reciprocated much of what I'd given. Swirling. Spearing my slit. His silky tongue against my sensitized skin. And then he used just a little bit of teeth, and I nearly came apart.

I tapped his shoulder. "Stop."

Immediately, he pulled off and gazed up. "Are you okay?"

Okay? I'm about to lose my ever-loving mind. "I want to come inside you."

He arched an eyebrow. "I thought you were about to."

I burst out laughing. "That's fair. I meant in your ass."

Licking his lips, he offered up a lascivious smile. "Oh, I want that too. We aren't in a rush, are we?"

"Uh." I swallowed. "Refractory periods are a thing, I'm afraid."

For a moment, my words hung in the air. "Oh."

"Yeah, I'm not eighteen anymore."

"Well, I'm not either." He tried to look offended. And failed miserably.

"There's a difference between twenty-nine and forty-five. At least I've found there is." I pointed to his already burgeoning erection. "That wouldn't happen to me. Not nearly that fast." Maybe not ever. Howard had been a one-and-done guy. Once we'd fucked, he'd go to sleep, and that was the end of it. No matter how much more I wanted. How much more I craved—he never indulged me. He'd scoff at my neediness, turn his back, and be snoring within minutes.

Arnav held my gaze. "Another time, though, right? Because I only got the smallest of tastes, and I definitely want more. Promise me?"

And because I could deny him nothing, I smiled. "I promise." I ran my hand through his silky black hair. "Now, we're both naked, and there's a perfectly good bed. Care to make use of it?"

He grinned. "You don't have to ask twice."

Chapter Fifteen

Arnav

Foster pulled down the sheet and comforter, but only far enough that I could get under them. I stole a long glance at his naked body as he joined me. His dark skin was a delicious contrast to the pale-blue sheets. In dissimilarity to my own paler body. So many shades and yet we were all the same. All human. In this moment, I was keenly aware of how divergent our lives had truly been.

He'd had a difficult childhood.

Mine had been easy.

He hadn't talked about what coming out had been like for him. Hell, I might've outed him on Friday night when I'd brushed a kiss to his cheek in Fifties. I mentally cursed myself for not having that conversation first.

I'd been out at a young age. And yeah, gotten lots of flak for being a twink. Being too femme. Being just too much in general. I'd reined some of that in when I'd gone to university and law school—but I'd also stayed true to who I was in private. And now I was about to be intimate with a guy who, in some respects, I barely knew. In other ways, I knew everything that mattered. His kind heart. His generous soul. His tortured past.

When he crawled on top of me, I opened my thighs to welcome him. He canted his hips so our cocks brushed. And yes, refractory periods weren't quite as big of a deal for me. I often was able to go again in just a short period of time. Would that change in the next sixteen years? Anatomy said yes. Aging said yes. My mind rebelled, though. Foster wasn't old. No matter how hard he tried to put that between the two of us, I wouldn't give in on that. Young at heart. That was the saying.

Right.

He pressed his lips to mine and all thoughts of age and bounce-back periods fled my mind.

I ran my hands from his broad shoulders, down his flanks, to his ass. I grasped the round firm cheeks and squeezed.

He moaned.

I coaxed him closer.

"Slow down." The panted words escaped his lips through labored breaths. "Remember, I want to be in you."

"So get in me." I squeezed his ass again. "Nothing's stopping you."

"Well...at the very least, I want to prep you." He rolled off me and headed toward the nightstand.

Patiently I waited. But once he had a condom wrapper and the lube in his hand, my patience ran out. I snagged the lube out of his fingers, opened my legs, and started prepping myself.

"Hey." He frowned.

"Next time, okay?" I stuck a couple of fingers into my ass and reveled in the burn. "Next time you can take all the time you want. This time? We're getting on with it right now."

He blinked. "Well, okay." He opened the condom wrapper, knelt, and rolled the condom on his impressive length. Long and slender. Great for nailing my prostate.

I tossed him the lube.

He grinned as he slathered himself.

"Who's in charge?" I eyed him.

After a moment's consideration, he answered, "You are."

"But you understand you can say *stop* at any time, right? That you're not obliged to do anything you don't want to?"

Slowly, he nodded. "Yeah, I get it."

"Great, then fuck me already."

A grin spread across his face. "Whatever you want."

I pulled my knees up and out of the way as he positioned himself between my thighs. As he guided himself to me, our gazes held.

He drew in a long, shaky breath. "I...uh..."

"I know." I said the words as softly as I could. Because I *did* know. Because I felt the same way. Although we'd only known each other four days—or four weeks, if one counted the blow job at Quinton's—I knew how I felt about him. I was looking at him and, as improbable as it felt, saw my future.

After a moment, he pressed into me.

I reveled in the burn as his crown pushed in. I loved sex, and I enjoyed the sensation of being filled. Of being connected. I saw my future.

He pulled his lower lip through his teeth as he continued to push in.

I wound my legs around his waist and pressed my heels into his ass.

He pushed deeper and, after a rather long period of time, bottomed out. He sighed.

"Great, now will you please fuck me into the mattress? I'm not fragile. Some guys might be, but—"

He withdrew and thrust back in.

I grunted. "Perfect. Now again."

To my delight, he obeyed my command. Over and over—with greater intensity and force, but letting me guide his rhythm and speed with my words.

Chasing my orgasm proved challenging as I worried about his frame of mind as much as my own.

"I need you to come." He said the words through gritted teeth.

"Huh?" I'd been so focused on him that the words were slow in registering.

"Please." He thrust in again. "Jerk yourself. Just...do something."

"Oh, right." Somehow that hadn't occurred to me. I grasped my shaft and tugged along to the rhythm he set. The added friction was enough to send me over the edge. "I'm coming." And with that, I erupted over my hand, with my cum going all over my chest, up my neck, hitting my chin, and even onto the sheets.

"Oh, thank fuck." He thrust twice more, then held himself still, his head thrown back.

As much as I wanted to command him to meet my stare, I faltered.

He let out a howl of pleasure.

A howl I felt from my tingling scalp down to the tips of my toes. Fuck, that was *hot*.

Slowly, he lowered his head and met my gaze. He blinked several times—whether to bring me into focus or to stave off tears, I wasn't certain.

So I opened my arms.

He lowered himself into my embrace, ignoring the mess of my spunk between us.

I might've been grateful he didn't just drop like a stone. He wasn't huge, but he had a bit of heft. All those muscles that had held him up as he'd drilled me good. I didn't always like to go so vigorous on my first go-round with a guy. With Foster, though, I had no worries. He'd treated me like the precious person he seemed to believe I was. Not china or anything, just...someone to be cared for.

And he'd listened so well. His submissive nature called to me. Not all pups were subs. Some were assertive, some were brats, and some—like Foster—were cuddle muffins. As I held him, he let his true nature show, smooshing his face in against my neck. I held him, stroked him, and even gave him little scritches.

In other words, I tried to show him just how damn much I cared.

And he reacted to my affection by holding me closer. His dick eased out of me with a little pop, but I barely felt it. After all these years, I knew how to prep myself. Knew exactly how much I could take. Sometimes I needed slow and sensual. Sometimes I needed passionate and life-affirming.

Well, we'd definitely affirmed life this afternoon.

"I must be heavy."

"I can manage." I held him tighter, but as his back cooled, we needed to either pull up the comforter or get up so we could clean ourselves. "Why don't you roll over? I'll clean us and then we can snuggle."

He raised his head. "You'd do that?"

I scratched his scalp in a way I'd noted he enjoyed.

He closed his eyes in evident bliss.

"We can do whatever you want."

"I need to dig your SUV out."

Ugh. He sort of had a point.

"Why don't we check the weather report? If the temperature is going to rise, maybe the snow will melt." Even I knew how absurd that notion was. Several feet of snow didn't melt in a few hours. Or even a day. Not unless the temperature shot up to a level it would never.

He chuckled. "Nice try. I agree to checking the weather report while you clean us. I like the idea of just lying here though."

"You do look sort of blissed. Or would you prefer your dog bed?" He might want to settle into relaxation that way. Maybe have a nap.

As he tucked his head against my neck, he whispered, "Thank you for understanding. I'm good, though. Just want to be with you."

Music to my ears. So I gently eased him off me and left him with his phone while I went to the washroom. I cleaned myself up, needed to piss—thanks to the two coffees—and then headed back into the bedroom with a warm washcloth.

He grinned as I wiped him down. He'd removed the condom and knotted it off, so I took it and the washcloth back to the bathroom.

When I returned, he held the comforter up for me.

I dove in. He hadn't been kidding when he said he kept the house cold. I didn't regret not taking my socks off. I might've looked less than elegant, but at least my feet were warm.

"The snow is going to stop in a couple of hours—according to the weather app, which is pretty reliable. The city says all the streets in Mission City proper should be plowed within the next hour or so."

He lay on his back, so I snuggled up against him, placing my head in the crook of his arm. "So we're good for a while yet."

"Yeah, I'd say so. Once the plow passes, it shouldn't take me long to dig you out. Then you can be on your way."

I didn't want to go. Honestly, I would've stayed if I could. Except I had a major client meeting in the morning, and as long as they were able to make it to my office, we were good. I could do a video conference, but I didn't like the impersonality of that. Sometimes it couldn't be helped. Most of the time, I managed to see people in the office. I also needed to prep for the meeting, and that couldn't be done on my phone alone.

Finally, although my mother was good at calming my father, he still worried. When I'd left for university, he tried to talk me into the hellacious commute to the University of British Columbia. I'd stood firm and lived in a dorm. When I'd finished law school, though, Papi was the one who had convinced me to move home. He left other aspects of mothering up to my mother, but he liked to keep me within reach at all times.

I'd been sending messages to the family group chat and endured serious ribbing since Rashmi had boldly told everyone I'd been out on a date when the snowstorm had stranded me.

Serious payback was in order.

"Arnav?"

"Yes?" I angled my head so I could meet his gaze.

"Are we going to do this again?"

I pushed up so I could drop a kiss to his lips. "I certainly hope so."

"Yeah. Okay. Me too." He pressed a kiss to my forehead.

Part of me wanted to encourage him to roll onto his side so I could spoon him. So I could protect him. The rest of me was reassured when his eyes drifted shut and he went to sleep.

He's comfortable enough with me to be vulnerable. That's a good sign.

Or he was just a guy who fell asleep after sex. Given what he'd said about his ex, though, that didn't seem likely. No, he trusted me.

That meant everything.

Chapter Sixteen

Foster

Much as I'd predicted, digging Arnav's SUV out of the snow proved easy. Well, for me. The snowplow had packed the slush in pretty compact, but I used a hoe to break it up and then a shovel to remove enough chunks so he could drive away.

We might've kissed a whole lot before he left.

He might've whispered he was going to give me a completed blow job the first chance he got.

I might've promised more steamy nights in our future. And I didn't mean I'd turn up the baseboard heater.

He left, and I pulled out my laptop. For Arnav, I could at least look.

Healing Horses Ranch.

Finding the counseling center's website proved easy. Clicking on each counselor and reading their bio was simple. Verifying my insurance covered all the therapists based on their qualifications was a breeze.

Figuring out what to do next was complicated.

Do I really need therapy? What if I go and someone else needs the spot more and I'm taking that from them? What if I can't say anything that makes sense? What if I just sit and cry for an hour?

Then I gave myself a stern talking to. Arnav wouldn't have suggested this if he didn't feel I might benefit. I'd seen how much it helped Gerry as he dealt with his kid's cancer.

I didn't have to tell anyone I was going. Not that I was embarrassed. Gerry told everyone he'd gone and how it'd made a difference. He wanted the other folks on the crew to know that getting help was a sign of strength, not a sign of weakness. He was my best framer. Worked his ass off. I'd poached him after he'd finished a project in Abbotsford, and he now worked on my crew. I counted on him.

He'd never let me down.

Just like I never wanted to falter with my crew. I'd come a long way since I'd been Howard's…plaything. I didn't look back fondly on those ten years. Ten fucking years. He'd moved on.

So had I.

Or so I told myself.

But every time I thought about Arnav—and the possibility of making things more serious—I flashed back to Howard. How I'd felt so lighthearted at the beginning. Had believed we had such promise. How I'd found my soulmate. Even how much he cared about me when he asked me to stop working. He'd said he wanted me to have an easy life. No more hard labor.

I hadn't seen the trap. Maybe because I wasn't the sharpest nail in the pile. Maybe because I wanted what he offered. What I'd only ever had with PJ—security. Well-being. Happiness.

All that had turned to shit, and yet I'd never found the strength to leave him. I'd kept believing things would get better.

They never had.

Because I hadn't fought back. That wasn't my nature.

And Howard had known that. Had exploited that. Had turned my life into a nightmare. The worst part was I'd still be living like that...if not for him booting me to the curb. With literally nothing.

I glanced around the house. I didn't own this place, but I'd fixed it up. Had put blood, sweat, and tears into doing the work. That sense of accomplishment sank deep into the marrow of my bones. Frank would need to rent it out at full market price soon. With all the work I'd done, he could fetch quite a lot for it. More than I could pay. My down payment fund was still anemic...but every month it increased. Maybe if I could find a room in a house and pay as little as I could, I might be able to save up faster.

The idea of sharing a house rankled. I didn't want people in my space—and I didn't want to be in theirs. I liked living alone.

You wouldn't mind living with Arnav.

Well, okay, that was true. He didn't make fun of me when I needed to sleep in my dog bed. He'd yet to see me as a full pup. From everything he'd said and done, though, I believed he'd be respectful. And rambunctious was beyond me. Sure, I liked playing. More, though, I liked to curl up and be petted.

Be loved.

And that was a hell of a leap with a guy I'd known for less than a week.

Except for the blow job.

Yeah, okay, that too.

An auspicious beginning. To a relationship I'd never seen coming. I hadn't thought I'd ever see Arnav again. Let alone at a puppy party in Vancouver. And I kept circling around to that. He'd chosen to be there. Clearly without any reservation. Obviously knowing what the night was about.

He chose you.

Yeah, he had. And I wanted to be worthy.

I found the phone number for Healing Horses Ranch and dialed. I could leave a message and hopefully someone would call me back tomorrow. This had to be done before I chickened—

"Healing Horses Ranch, this is Rainbow, how may I help you?"

I nearly dropped the phone. "Uh, hello?"

"Hi. How are you today?"

"Surprised you answered the phone."

"Ah, you thought you'd leave a message and someone would get back to you tomorrow?" She laughed. "I have a bad habit of grabbing the phone whenever it rings. Since I live and work on the ranch, it's kind of all smooshed together." She paused. "But I can hang up, you can call back, and you can leave a message."

"No." *For God's sake, you're an adult. Speak.* "I...I don't remember seeing you on the list of counselors."

Another laugh. "Oh, I'm not. I'm the manager. I wrangle horses, dogs, and therapists." She paused, as if letting that sink in. "Do you know which counselor you'd like to see? Everyone has different availabilities—"

"Soon." I took a breath. "I mean it's not urgent and I'm, like, okay. Just...a friend suggested I might benefit from talking to someone. Someone other than him. I don't think he minds, but I think he believes a therapist might be a better sounding board. Does that sound right?"

"It does. You don't have to tell me your issue, but was there someone in particular?"

"Like…" I drew in a deep breath. "I'm gay. And…kinky?" Okay, that was the first time I'd ever referred to myself that way.

"Okay, no worries. Kennedy has several clients who live alternative lifestyles. Justin is gay. Not giving anything away—he's upfront about that. Avery has also seen queer clients. Denise focuses on children, so she's not likely who you want to see."

"No, for sure not." I pulled my lower lip through my teeth. "Does Justin have an opening?"

"He does." The sound of her typing on a keyboard came through clearly. "He's got a cancellation tomorrow night. Does six o'clock work?"

"Evenings?" Somehow, I'd assumed the counselors only worked days.

"Yes. Everyone takes a turn doing an evening shift. We recognize not everyone can get here during the day. If daytime is better, he's got an opening on a Wednesday next month—"

"No. Sorry, didn't mean to cut you off."

She laughed. "Oh, no worries. I'm here to help you. To figure out what would work best for you."

"Tomorrow night at six works. Just…I won't have time to shower after work."

"We're a working ranch. Well, we have horses, hay, and, this time of year, plenty of mud and snow. In fact, I'm offering this appointment, but I should be checking to see if you have snow tires. Our street was just plowed, and we've got a woman we hire who does our driveway, but it might still be slippery."

"Pickup truck with snow tires."

"Then you should be fine. No more snow in the forecast." She typed something else. "If you're comfortable, you can give me your email address, and I can send you the intake form. If you're able to fill it out and email it back, Justin can read it and have some idea of what's going on. Or you can just come in. Oh, what's your name?"

"Foster."

"That's a lovely name. You know I'm Rainbow. Justin's last name is Bridges."

I'd seen that on the website, but I appreciated her taking the time to let me know. His photo wasn't on the website, so I had no idea what he looked like. *Guess I'll find out tomorrow.* "Uh, email." I rattled it off.

She repeated it and then, as if by magic, her email arrived in my inbox. "Now, if you've got questions, you're better off emailing them. I'm heading out to feed the horses, and I can't be certain Kennedy will hear the phone. I'm trying to encourage her to take time off every so often."

"Hazards of the job?"

"Living and working in the same place? For sure." She paused. "Oh, how are you with dogs? We can keep them out of the way—"

"I love dogs. Truly." *I like to pretend to be one.*

"That's great. I think Tiffany will be available, if you want her in your session. She's the official therapy dog. Rex, Avery's dog, is the unofficial one. He loves people, but sometimes takes a bit of time to warm up to strangers, which doesn't work for a therapy dog. Still, he's a sweetheart. But he won't be here tomorrow night. So, Tiffany's okay?"

"Uh, yeah, that would be wonderful."

"Awesome. If you can email the form back along with any questions, that would be great. General instructions including directions are included. Again, if you have a question, just ask."

"Thank you." I blinked. "This was way easier than I thought it would be."

"It's meant to be easy. Asking for help can be tough. You were brave and took the first step. Let us help you. Okay, Foster?"

"Yes, that would be nice. Uh, thanks." Then I hung up before I could rattle off a third thanks. Appreciation mixed with relief washed over me.

Diligently, I completed the intake form and read all the documentation about the ranch. Truthfully, the place sounded lovely. Serene. Friendly. And when I searched for reviews outside of their website, I spotted many positive ones. Along with a couple of negatives, but I didn't mind that. I usually worried if a place was too perfect.

Arnav.

He felt, at times, almost too perfect. And that thought led me to do what I should've done days ago.

I searched him.

And was reassured the professional reviews were mostly positive. Except one person who'd clearly been on the losing end of a confrontation with the lawyer with whom I was falling for. Hard and fast. So unexpected.

Yet I had very few worries and precisely zero regrets.

Chapter Seventeen

Arnav

"Took you long enough."

My Papi glared at me. The *dad* glare.

"He's a big boy." Mama pointed to my chair.

"I should help."

Rashmi poked my arm. "When do you ever help?"

"Hey!" I glared.

She snickered.

"Maybe I want to learn."

At my declaration, everyone stopped moving.

Mama, who stood at the stove, stopped stirring.

My father, who'd been carrying the container with the naan bread to the table, halted in his tracks.

Rashmi gaped.

Beena snickered. Kindly, her twin twelve-year-old daughters—my beloved nieces—just stared at me, as if not understanding what I'd said. Luckily, her husband was working. Otherwise, I would've gotten a disapproving look. Most of my sisters had married progressive husbands who contributed to the child rearing. Beena had chosen and married a man steeped in the old ways—and she was incredibly happy.

I held out my hands. "What?"

My mother put her hand on her hip. "And why haven't you told us about this man?"

"Uh, what man?"

Rashmi didn't even have the decency to keep in the laugh. "The man you've seen every night since Wednesday? The one whose house you stayed at last night?"

"I might've stayed over at Everett's." I was throwing my fellow lawyer and good friend under the bus, but my relationship with Foster felt too new. Too precarious. Too precious.

"Although Everett is handsome—and Black—he wasn't the man you kissed in Fifties on Friday night." My father gazed at me over his spectacles.

My jaw dropped at his comment. "And how do you know that?"

Rashmi snickered. She seemed to be doing that more than usual. And always at my expense.

"I was at the library yesterday morning, and that nice librarian..." He tapped his chin in contemplation.

"Loriana, Marnie, or Johanna?" Beena snagged the plate of naan.

"Loriana." He grinned. "Lovely woman."

"Yes." And recently married to a hunky man who knew his way around computers. I'd hired Mitch to fix my glitchy laptop because I didn't want to break in a new one. He'd done a bang-up job.

"Anyway." Papi walked back to the stove and took the bowl of rajma from Mom. "She asked me how you and Foster met." He placed the bowl on the table.

My saliva glands kicked into high gear. I'd have offered to bring food to the table, but my parents had enjoyed this routine since the earliest days of their marriage. One cooked and one brought the food to the table. My sisters had all taken their turn at learning the routine.

To my utter shame, I never had. I could whip up a few things in my kitchen downstairs, but only a few. French toast was truly the best I could do. Why bother to learn when I could sneak up here and steal leftovers whenever I wanted?

"She mentioned Foster by name?"

"Yes." He made his way back to the counter where Mama had put a large bowl of rice. "She said he'd been in the library once, and..." He frowned. "Oh, right, Marnie had spoken to him. Loriana noted it because Marnie's shy, and she was under the impression Foster was as well."

Curiosity welled within me. Why had Foster gone to the library? A perfectly normal thing to do, but obviously he'd garnered some attention from the librarians. Well, Loriana did have a way with people. And apparently a big mouth. "What did you say to her?"

My father again looked at me over his spectacles. "I believe I said, *Foster? Who?*" He laughed. "She might've been a little flustered." He placed the rice before Beena, handed her the spoon, and indicated she should start dishing out the food.

She obliged.

"I said I had no idea who Foster was, but that obviously my son would share that information with me. Especially given how small Mission City is and how gossip spreads."

Slowly, heat crept into my cheeks.

"Is this the same handsome man you had dinner with at Stavros's?" Rashmi batted her eyelashes as she took the rice from Beena.

"Okay, how...?"

"Timothea is friends with Ravi. You know, the nurse?"

"Yes, I know Ravi." He was married to Maddox, they had two kids, and he worked in the pediatric department at the hospital.

"Well, Timothea ran into Ravi at the drug store. They got to talking, and she mentioned this cute gay couple and, of course, she assumed he knew them because he's gay, and...well...you know..."

"Yes. All the gay men know all the gay men in Mission City. Big assumption for a town that size." The city was still considered a small town, despite its name. But with the continual growth—and as a major supplier of workers who commuted to the large city of Vancouver—our town kept growing. Hence Foster having work building houses. What had once been an affordable city was now getting beyond the reach of many—therefore driving the need for below-market rentals.

Rashmi waved her fork like a weapon. "So you admit there's a guy."

"I don't think I was trying to deny it." Except I totally had been—but she was just too easy to rile.

"Children." Mama snapped the word as she sat at the head of the table.

Papi sat at the other end.

"Uncle Arnav has a boyfriend." Aliyah grinned.

"I didn't say that."

Mishka waved her fork—much like her aunt had. "But you love him." She put heavy emphasis of the *o*.

Frankly, I'd been amazed they'd been so silent through the grilling part of this. Maybe when their grandparents sat down, they saw that as permission to pile on their favorite uncle.

Okay, their only uncle. At least on their mother's side. Well, I had a pile of brothers-in-law, and they were all uncles.

So I was their favorite uncle. I made my play. "What if I did have a boyfriend?" The rice finally made its way to me, and I put some on my plate.

Aliyah squealed.

Mishka rolled her eyes.

Rashmi snickered. "You'd better admit it—the entire town's talking about it."

I shifted. "I don't...I don't know if he wants to be talked about. No, scratch that. I do know. He's an intensely private man."

"At least he's a man." Mama waved her hand around. "Better than those *boys* you've been dating."

I just sat there.

Slack-jawed.

Then I narrowed my eyes at Rashmi.

She shrugged. "You're the one with the second social media account under the fake name. You thought I wouldn't find it? I might've been laughing, and Mama might've—"

"Oh my God."

"Hey." Papi narrowed his eyes. "I got a good look too. Were they even legal?"

I tried to gesture at my nieces with my chin.

Beena laughed. "You think they don't know everything? They figured out Instagram before I did."

Rashmi and Beena were also twins and couldn't have been more different. Rashmi was all about the latest trends, fashions, and gadgets. She'd been living quite the high life in Vancouver until she'd come home after the divorce. Beena had stuck close to home until she'd met a man who liked traditional roles. They suited each other. Sometimes, though, I thought Rashmi had an outsized influence on our nieces. I'd yet to determine if that was good or not.

"Be that as it may..." I scrunched my nose. "I like him. I really like him. I don't want the family bulldozing over him."

"Hey." Every person at the table—every single one—said the word in unison.

"I think you just made my point rather effectively. Snooping in my personal life, gossiping with everyone about me." And how, even though I did it accidentally, how outing Foster could have an impact on him beyond what I'd imagined. How much might my family's gossip hurt him? With his job? With his emotional state? We hadn't really talked about that and now, apparently, my family was talking about nothing but. *You did this. You kissed him on the cheek. This is on you.* I might've been furious with my family, but I was more ashamed at my own actions. Inadvertent as they might've been.

My words set off cross talk between my parents, my sisters, and my nieces. All going on and on about how gentle our family could be. I heard the word *non-intrusive* and nearly peed my pants I laughed so hard. My family had been all up in my business since the day I'd been born. They shouldn't, though, be up in Foster's.

And I loved them despite it.

Wouldn't trade them for anything or anyone.

But will Foster want to be part of this chaos? Can we be together and he not see them? Be around them? Run into them in town? I had no doubt a picture of him would be shared in the group chat as soon as one became available. And then all bets were off.

"I think we should have the young man over for dinner." Mama gestured to the table. "Just the four of us."

Rashmi started to protest.

Papi cut her a look.

"Or you can invite him for Christmas. That's less than a month away. That will give you time to *prepare* him."

She does not know what prepare means with gay men, and you're not going to laugh.

I didn't.

But came damn close.

"Christmas? You think exposing him to that chaos is the right thing to do?"

"Not that anyone wants my opinion—" Rashmi glared at everyone sitting at the table. "—but I think it's the perfect time. With..." She counted on her hands repeatedly.

I interrupted, "Six sisters, five brothers-in-law, eleven nephews, seven nieces, and parents who don't know how to mind their own damn business?" *See? I pay attention. Everyone thinks I don't...but I do.*

Aliyah clapped. "Well done."

I glared. "See if I get you anything for Christmas."

She grinned impishly. "I know you love me."

"Well...maybe."

"But someone's love is not demonstrated by whether or not they buy you a gift." Papi pointed to Aliyah.

"I know." Her grin didn't diminish. "Because, when times are tough, love is all we have."

"And family," Mishka piped up.

Beena appeared quite proud of her daughters.

And herself.

Rashmi smirked.

I rolled my eyes.

"Invite him." Mama took her turn pointing her fork. "He has free will. He can always say *no*."

But he wouldn't. I knew this down to the depths of my soul—if I asked him, he would come. But was I pushing too hard? I seemed to always be running roughshod over him. Pushing him out of his comfort zone. Encouraging him to face tough stuff from his past. What gave me the right to do that? I didn't have trauma. Hadn't gone through a hundredth of what he had. Had never faced parental rejection. Hadn't been through the foster system. Certainly hadn't been in an abusive relationship. So where did I come off telling him what to do? Recommending therapy? Not my place.

And yet I had. I'd suggested getting help might be good. Would he understand I was only making a suggestion? Or would he think I was insisting because I was his Daddy?

Daddy. That was a tremendous amount of responsibility. Was I up for that? I'd never done this long term. Despite my protestations, I was still young. Still green. I could go on instinct, but I couldn't fix him.

Much as I wanted to.

"I'll see about inviting him." *You'll also have to explain how you still live with your parents. Awkward...*

He's worth it. He's absolutely worth it.

So I'd ask.

And pray my family doesn't scare him off.

Chapter Eighteen

Foster

As I sat on the couch in Justin Bridges's office, a calm settled over me. Tiffany, the yellow lab, sat by my legs. She'd greeted me with great enthusiasm when I arrived. And had stuck to my side as Rainbow had given me a tour of the facilities. The ranch looked wonderful—with the barn, stables, riding ring, and forest just behind. I wanted to come back in the daylight to get a full sense of the place.

Justin's office was a bright yellow. Soothing. He was soothing as well. The bearded ginger was pretty solidly built as well. And had the most amazing smile. Despite myself, I felt at ease.

"You said on your form that you want to talk about your childhood." Justin smiled. "That's absolutely fine. I just want to get a quick understanding of where you are and why you've decided now would be a good time to dig into your past."

"Are you thinking I shouldn't?"

"No, far from it. We're here to do whatever works for you. If you want to dive straight into your past, that's not a problem. I was more hoping to get a sense of what your goals are for coming here." He sipped from his mug of tea.

I gripped a bottle of water Rainbow had given me. "I guess... Well, I've met someone. And that's brought all kinds of stuff up. Because he's a great guy, and I want to be the best person I can with him." I rubbed my eyes with my hand. "I kind of broke down, and he gently suggested Healing Horses."

"Oh." Justin scratched his beard. "We always appreciate referrals."

"Arnav Mehta." I winced. "I've discovered that a whole pile of people know about the two of us. One dinner at Stavros's and one night at Fifties and apparently, we're the new *it* couple in Mission City." Vivi, no less, had told me. She was friends with someone whose name I forgot but who was friends with Sarabeth from Fifties and wow, hadn't it been sweet that Arnav had kissed me? Oh, and Vivi hadn't known I was gay or bi or whatever, but that was awesome too, and her sister was a lesbian, and...

I was out. Quietly. Without much fanfare. And not one person on the site had said anything. We'd all just done our jobs.

Justin shifted. "I know Arnav. Quite well. He's...a good man."

"He's the best." I petted Tiffany's head as she placed her chin on my knees. "We met at Club Kink."

"I'm familiar with the club. I haven't been there myself, but Kennedy has counseled several members over the years. I'm open to hearing about all kinds of lifestyles. Truly, I don't judge. As you read, though, if I hear of a child being abused, I have to report that."

I'd read the paperwork. And how if I was a danger to myself or others that he'd have to report that as well. I liked that he was watching out for people. That gave me comfort.

"No children. No abuse. Just..." I bit my lower lip. "Okay, this stays between us, right? You'll never say anything?"

He nodded. "My relationship with Arnav is legal and professional. He and I say things that I wouldn't share with you. Whatever's said in this office stays here."

"So Arnav and I met at Quinton's Halloween party."

Justin's eyebrow arched. "My husband and I missed that. My daughter had a fever. She was fine by the next day, but there was no way we'd leave her with a babysitter."

Which reassured me. "I, uh, hooked up with Arnav."

"Okay." He held my gaze with stunning sky-blue eyes that were clearly curious.

"Yeah, I...might've given him a blow job." I pushed that out really fast. "In Quinton's spare room, and then I heard someone in the hall, and I panicked, and I ran." I gazed up at the stucco ceiling and noted the solid construction that I'd spotted in the main room carried through here. The room where I entered was two stories high, with wood beams and floor-to-ceiling windows that probably let in a ton of light during the day. Justin's office also had big windows, and they looked out over the parking lot, and—

"Are you embarrassed about how you...hooked up?"

I blew out a breath, said a little prayer, and met his gaze. "I was. Truly. I'd had a couple of quick hookups in my twenties, but I was in the closet, so nothing ever came of them. I was in a serious relationship for all of my thirties. A clusterfuck we can unpack at some future time. I got dumped and had to start life all over again. With literally nothing.

And I plodded along, never thinking about guys because I was so damn busy trying to get my feet under me. Then I met Quinton."

Justin chuckled. "He's...something."

"He's amazing." I sighed. "He saw a lonely guy—quite possibly queer—and he invited that guy to a Halloween party. And that guy found the courage to go. And he met the most beautiful man, and..." I shrugged and sort of smiled. "I don't know what happened. I don't recognize the man who went upstairs with Arnav and gave him a blow job. Now, the man who ran away? Him, I recognize."

"Do you still?"

I cocked my head.

"Are you still the man who ran? Are you comfortable being out of the closet?"

After a long moment, I shrugged. "I know he didn't mean to out me. He didn't know. And a simple peck on the cheek shouldn't have caused the stir it did." I considered. "But I also didn't wipe my cheek and brush him off. I invited him to my house. Because of the snowstorm, his SUV was out front for more than a day. Any one of my neighbors could've seen it."

Justin shifted. "I'm not certain you've answered my question."

I sat a little straighter. "I don't care. I'm forty-five fucking years old. Was in what amounted to an abusive relationship for ten years where I barely left the house, let alone the closet. Why should I keep hiding who I am? Who am I protecting? Myself? No, I'm not. By hiding who I am, I'm actually hurting myself. If people don't like it, then that's on them."

He ran a hand over his mouth.

"I'm amusing you, aren't I?" I wasn't the least bit offended. "Oh, and sorry about the language."

"I've heard that and much worse. We have several friends in common and, when little ears aren't around to hear, I'd say curse words are pretty common."

Figuring out who we knew in common would be interesting. I had so few friends. But he knew Quinton. And had he said something about Ravi and Maddox? They'd been at the party. Amazing how similar Justin and Maddox were in appearances. "Is it going to be a problem? That we know some of the same people?"

He shook his head. "No one needs to know you're here. I'll keep my distance if we wind up somewhere at the same time. Like a social event or just around town."

"And maybe I won't need too many sessions..."

"That's entirely possible."

My phone buzzed in my back pocket.

I winced. "Sorry, it might—"

He waved me off. "Life happens."

Still, I was chagrinned as I yanked it out and quickly checked the screen.

—I know this is sudden, and I should probably ask in person...but my family wanted me to invite you to Christmas. I figured the more time you had to prepare, the better it would be. No pressure. I plan to see you lots before that. Uh...later. —

"Well, okay, then."

Justin cocked his head.

I drew in a deep breath and let it out slowly. "Arnav just invited me to his family's Christmas dinner. Isn't it, like, soon?"

"Christmas is just over four weeks away—"

"I meant that we've only seen each other five times in total. Barely exchanged any texts."

"Ah." He offered a smile. "You can always say *no*."

The phone in my hand felt like a dead weight. "I don't know…"

"What's your gut reaction?"

"Hell fucking yes." I blinked. "That makes no sense, right? Just because he makes me feel good about myself. Just because he accepts I like to sleep in a dog bed and enjoy scritches as much as kisses. Just because we've had sex—I mean super great awesome sex—doesn't mean I should meet his family…right?"

"I don't normally talk about myself. That's not a therapist's role. But anyone in our circle can tell you that Stanley and I met Christmas Eve and were committed to each other by New Year's Eve. Now, were there issues to work out? Certainly. Did we have someone else relying on us? Yep. That made it even more important that we not be impetuous. That we do things properly. Yet he made the decision to sell his place in Vancouver and move to Mission City in the blink of an eye. Not just for me, to be sure, but us getting together factored into it. I told my parents back east about him. And the reason we'd met."

Which had me intensely curious, but that curiosity would have to go unsated because, yeah, none of my damn business. I could guess, given they had children, but I couldn't be certain.

"Well, I don't have family. So that's a non-issue. He's got six older sisters. I can't even fathom that."

"Are you worried about being judged?"

"Of course they're going to judge me. He's the baby of the family—he said so himself. That's a lot of pressure on me. To be good enough for him."

"There is another option."

"What?"

"You know, they might love you. If they see the man I do—clearly compassionate, kind, and caring—then they might just think you're good enough for their son and brother. And so what if they don't?

Arnav has clearly made his decision. And made his choice clear to his family. They've invited you. Also, you might ask to meet his parents first. Or one or two sisters. You don't have to do the entire clan at once."

"Or I can just bite the bullet."

He laughed. "Not the analogy I would've chosen. That would be hard on your teeth. But I get what you're saying. And you're right—there's something to be said about just going. Do you want to go?"

Slowly, I nodded. "Yeah, I do."

"We have enough time to talk about your past, if you think that will still be helpful. Or I can help you prepare for your future."

"Uh...both?"

"Absolutely." He offered a wide grin. "Now, why don't you tell me about your pup. Do you have a name?"

I blinked. "A dog name?"

He nodded. "Some pups choose special names. Some just use their own name. Entirely up to you." He tilted his head. "I'm trying to say I'm glad you've found something that makes you happy. If Arnav accepts that part of you, it can be a special way for you two to connect."

"He's said he'll be my Daddy. When we role play."

"I think that's a great idea. Daddies can make us feel safe. Can accept us for who we are. Help us reach our full potential."

That sounded pie-in-the-sky to me.

But I'd take it and hold on tight.

"So let me tell you why I chose to be a pup."

And we were off.

Chapter Nineteen

Arnav

Four weeks flew by.

A big case landed in my lap. A guy accused of defrauding the company he worked for. Serious charges were levied against him.

He swore he hadn't done it.

To my frustration, the case was set to go to court in the new year, and the guy's attorney had dropped him as a client. Okay, she had good personal reasons, but that left the accused flapping in the wind with a judge who wasn't happy about any type of delay.

So I worked like a dog to get the mess sorted.

My job was to try to prove him innocent. I hired a local accountant, Darius Evans, to take a look at the evidence.

He spent two weeks tearing everything apart.

And, in the end, he figured out what the problem was.

Or rather, who the problem was.

On December twenty-first, I took the evidence to an assistant crown prosecutor. I'd always found Remy Stevens to be a level-headed woman who would hear all the facts before passing judgment. She wasn't the prosecutor on the case. So, my approaching her was, like, marginally unethical. Certainly unorthodox. But the prosecutor on the case wouldn't listen.

Remy did.

Two days later, the charges against my client were dropped. And the business's accounting clerk was arrested. A very clever accounting clerk. Who almost got away with close to half a million dollars.

The exonerated man thanked me, Darius, Remy, and anyone else who he could. And he was free of the burden he'd carried for so long.

On December twenty-fourth, I sat in Foster's kitchen. He frowned. "It's Christmas Eve—you should be home with your family."

I grasped his hand. "You've been so patient. We've barely seen each other. My family will understand."

"You've barely seen them either."

Now would probably be a good time to tell him you live with them. I took a deep breath. "Okay, so here's where I come clean about something."

He arched an eyebrow. "Am I going to like this, or are we talking shock level? I have Justin on speed dial."

I loved how he could joke about his therapist. He'd shared a few words about each session with me, and I was so glad Justin was helping. Sometimes Mission City felt small, as I'd helped Justin and Stanley such a short time ago. But they were no longer my clients, so that felt less like a conflict. "Uh, no, you won't need Justin." I winced. "Just...you know how I haven't invited you to my place yet?"

He laughed. "Well, you've been saving the *meet the parents* moment for Christmas Day. A little over-the-top, but I worked through my issues with Justin. I don't blame you for not inviting me over."

I blinked. "You know I live with my parents?"

"Well, Nadia told me how she delivers groceries to your family, and isn't it convenient that you live there and can help put everything away? I didn't realize your parents were quite so..."

"Don't say old. I only put away the really heavy stuff. They're spry for their age, trust me. I wouldn't recommend using old, elderly, or any other word like that—whether in their presence or just with some random stranger who works at the grocery store." Of course, given how gossipy they were, I shouldn't really be suggesting he do anything that considerate of them.

He frowned. "She's not a stranger. To either of us. I don't know who told her about our relationship..."

I closed my eyes for a brief moment. "Any one of about three dozen people. My family alone covers massive amounts of territory." I squeezed his hand. "I didn't mean to out you. And I'm sorry for that."

"I'm not." He offered me his shy smile. "I didn't come out because I didn't have a reason to. No one who'd captured my heart. My imagination. And yes, I could've come out to represent and to show that not everyone working in the trades is straight...but I just didn't feel the need to put myself out there like that. But with you..." He swallowed and squeezed my hand back. "You make me want to be a better person. And if that means being out and proud, then I'm all for that. A woman on my crew came to talk to me. Her son is trans, and he's struggling, and she wondered if I'd talk to him. I mean, I said *sure*, but what do I know about being trans?

"But the kid just needed to know he was not alone. And he's going to talk to Justin. I let his mom know that our insurance would cover the cost. So that was good, right? That never would have happened. And if that boy finds acceptance, then I've done something right." He blinked. "So, yeah. No regrets."

I was bursting with pride. All that had happened, and I'd been so wrapped up in work that I hadn't even known. "That's great, Foster. I'm not using this patronizingly—but I'm really proud of you."

"Oh." He ducked his head.

I placed my finger under his chin and guided him up to meet my gaze. "Own it, pup."

He nodded, blinking several times.

"Now, we have the evening to ourselves. What would you like to do?"

"Watch a movie?" His eyes shone.

Since I'd practically moved my entire rom-com collection over, he had plenty to pick from. Or... "Is there a Christmas movie you'd like to see? Something with a dog?"

"Oh." He held my gaze. "I love *Beethoven's Christmas Adventure*. I own it."

"I have to admit I haven't seen that. But I'm looking forward to it. Are you going to lay in my lap?" He didn't actually lie in my lap, obviously, but he curled up on the couch next to me and put his head in my lap. I'd stroke him as we watched the movie. Despite our proximity—or rather his face near my private parts—I never got hard. These were the tender moments he needed.

Ones I'd come to crave myself.

"Oh yes. Then we can watch an adult movie...if you want."

I eyed him. "You realize that *Die Hard* is the best Christmas movie ever, right?"

"I've never seen it." He gazed at me with questioning eyes.

"Okay, well then, first we'll watch Beethoven and then we'll enjoy Bruce Willis. With Alan Rickman and Bonnie Bedelia."

"Sounds great."

We did just that. With his head in my lap, we watched the antics of a Saint Bernard. At least I thought the dog was a Saint Bernard. Cute as all hell—talking and such.

Foster laughed numerous times—including before the joke a couple of times. Clearly, he'd watched this movie often.

The second movie had him cowering behind his hands at several key moments. I worried he might be upset, but he also laughed a couple of times and cheered when Alan Rickman died the most epic of deaths.

When the credits rolled, he pushed himself into a sitting position with his hand braced against my knee. "Thank you, Daddy."

'Whatever makes you happy, pup."

He bit his lower lip. He did that quite often, and part of me wondered if I should point it out, and the rest of me decided that if worrying his lip was his worst habit, then we were doing okay.

"What is it?" Clearly he had something on his mind.

"Could we, uh..."

I caressed his cheek and scratched his stubble—just the way he liked it. "We can do whatever you like." We'd made love a couple of times over the last few weeks—when I'd specifically carved out time for him—but that had been a challenge in and of itself.

"I'd like a name." He nudged his chin up in defiance.

Holding back my grin took effort. This was something serious to him, and I needed to treat it as such. "Okay." I scratched his scalp.

He closed his eyes in obvious ecstasy.

Making him feel good was so very easy. I loved that about him. His calm affection. His gentle nature. That someone took advantage of that for years still caused anger to roil inside of me. From what Foster reported of his sessions with Justin, he was moving past the pain. Was embracing what I offered. "Have you thought about a name?"

His eyes popped open at my softly spoken question.

He ducked his head.

I waited.

Finally, he faced me. "Owners pick their pup's name. Handlers, I mean."

"We're companions." We still struggled for the right word.

"Daddies." He held himself still. "Daddies pick their pup's name."

My chest flooded with warmth. He was gaining confidence in using the word. The word that suited our relationship when we were like this. "Okay, how about, I don't know, Jojo?"

He cocked his head as if considering it. Then he slowly shook his head.

"Tripper?"

"Sounds like I'm always underfoot."

"Which you are definitely not." I smiled. "How about Pickle Fry? My friend had a dog with that name when we were growing up."

He wrinkled his nose. Definitely not. "Did you have a dog growing up?"

I shook my head. "Seven kids in sixteen years—my parents were busy."

His dark-brown eyes showed sorrow. I didn't bother to ask him about a pet. He never spoke of his time with his mother, which I respected. He was opening up more and talking about his good two years with Papa John. PJ had provided a solid upbringing and everything that comprised the Foster I knew—strong work ethic, huge compassion, caring for others, gentle to the core, and very playful—appeared to have come from his time in that wonderful foster home. Now, through his discussions with Justin, he was piecing things together. Stitching the good into a solid blanket that enveloped him.

Along with me. Or so I hoped. He said as much—when we found time to talk. "Okay, what are you thinking?"

"I kind of like Rusty." He squeezed my knee.

"Uh, you remember I told you about that lawyer? Remy?"

He nodded.

"Her husband's name is Rusty. And he's sort of well-known in the Cedar Valley community. We might get confused, even though I'd never use your name in public."

"Ah, well that's a *no*."

"How about…" I hesitated.

He prompted me by nodding.

"Sparky?"

He cocked his head.

"Bear with me. Sparky is joy. Sparky is curious. Sparky has a playful side. But Sparky can also take things seriously when he has to. He takes care of himself and watches out for others. He gives great snuggles and the best kisses."

He blinked. "I think I like Sparky."

I took his cheeks between my hands and pulled him in for a kiss. "I love Sparky." Our lips touched. Gently. Reverently.

"What?" He pulled back and gazed at me with startled eyes.

"Uh…" *Shit*. "Well, you know…"

"You love me? Or do you just love Sparky? Or the idea of Sparky? Because—"

I held up my hand.

He desisted.

"I said that wrong."

His face fell.

"No. Jesus, I'm not getting this right. It's late." I rubbed my eyes. "I meant to keep it to myself for a bit. We haven't even been together and a month, and—"

"Do you love me?" He stared at me—wary and a little hopeful.

"Yes."

He let out a breath.

My heart sank at his silence. "But you don't—"

"I love you too." He threw himself into my arms. "I wanted to tell you but, like you said, it's so soon. And the last time I did that, well..."

"I understand." We didn't discuss Howard often. Just sometimes when Foster came home from his counseling sessions and had some revelation he felt he needed to share with me. I'd listen attentively—because that's what good partners did—but I seethed on the inside. Foster, as if sensing my enmity, asked me not to track Howard down. That they'd parted and moved on with their lives. With Foster living in Cedar Valley and Howard being an important architect in Vancouver, their paths weren't likely to cross again. "This time's not going to follow that painful path."

"I'm old, Arnav. I'm only getting older—"

I glared. "First, you're not old. You're distinguished. You have life experience I can only begin to fathom. You can share the wisdom you've learned with your greener partner."

He arched an eyebrow.

"I'm serious. Look, your age has *never* been a factor with me."

He rolled his eyes.

"Hey."

His gaze shot to mine.

"If you won't look down on me for my age and inexperience, then why would I pass judgement on you and the choices you've made? They make you who you are. The man I love. Age is truly just a number. I hope you're going to have another forty-five years—and that they're all with me. Shit happens in life, Foster. Something might happen to me—"

He blinked.

"Or we're going to go along for decades and be fine. I like the idea that you're going to retire before me and live a life of resplendence and doggie spas while I'm working hard."

"I don't have much of a pension. Ten years out of the workforce..." He swallowed. "I really empathize with women who take time off to raise their kids."

"And fathers too."

"Of course." He winced. "That's beyond my experience. But I see Justin, and he's a great dad."

I sobered. "Do you want kids?"

"I'm way too old."

"That wasn't what I asked. Look, you know that Justin and Stanley were my clients. I'm sure Stanley won't mind me telling you that he became a father when he was older than you. He never planned to have kids. He told me as much—and not in a confidential way. We were talking at a party. His life turned upside down, and he has zero regrets. That tragedy—his brother dying—gave him a nephew who he adopted. And brought Justin into his life. They've made a beautiful family." I smiled.

He pulled his lower lip through his teeth for the half-dozenth time tonight. I was making him think about a lot of important things. Somehow this felt super important. Because, for some people, things like this were deal-breakers.

"Do you...?" He swallowed. "Do you want kids?"

I tried to read the correct answer in his expression, but he was doing a damn good job of keeping his expression neutral. I owed him honesty. "My six sisters have done a great job increasing the world's population. Well, except Rashmi. I adore my nieces and nephews. Would lay my life on the line for each of them. Would take over their care if that ever became necessary." I blew out a breath. "But that's not where I'm at for myself. I don't want to say I'm selfish—I donate money to charity, volunteer my time when I have it, drive an electric vehicle, and am careful with my carbon footprint. I want to leave the best world I can for the kids.

"But I don't want kids of my own. Now, if you have a burning desire to have them, then that's a negotiation we can enter into. I'm not averse to it—"

"You just said you don't want kids of your own."

"Uh..." Slowly, I nodded. "True. But I don't want to dictate the parameters of the relationship. If you have a strong desire—a need—for kids, then we can have that discussion."

Slowly, he nodded. "I don't. Want kids. I build houses for families with kids who need a home. I also donate time teaching kids about how to get into the trades. But I'm pretty sure I'd be a shitty dad."

"Foster—"

He shook his hand. "Part of me wants to be just like PJ. To make a difference in kids' lives. To have that kind of an impact. But I recognize that's not me. Justin and I talked about this. And he said some of what Stanley told you. He always knew he wanted to be a dad. He had that burning need. I don't...and he told me that was okay. I thought maybe foster kids. Older, you know? But I don't want to go through all that's involved." He held my gaze. "I like the relationship we have, and that would change if we had a young person in the house. I want to be your pup. To be the best pup ever. Maybe that's selfish, but that's also enough for me."

I smiled, pressing a hand to his cheek. "Are you sure?"

"Yes." He nodded emphatically.

"Well, after tomorrow, if you had any doubts, you'll know one way or the other."

He cocked his head.

"Seventeen kids ranging in age from seventeen to toddler."

His eyes widened.

I laughed. "I did warn you."

"Yeah, you did." He straightened his spine. "I'm sure I'll cope just fine."

I believed him. I really did. After a moment, I drew in a deep breath. "I have something to ask you."

He cocked his head. "You can ask me anything."

"This is big, Foster. And you need to know two things."

He nodded.

"First, that you can say *no*. No for now, or no forever."

His brow furrowed.

"The second thing is that you don't have to answer me now, okay? In fact, I'd almost prefer you didn't. Take you time, okay? This is a big decision."

"You're scaring me."

"I'm asking you to move in with me." I rushed out the words. I didn't mean my parents' place, of course. But somewhere we could call our own.

"May I answer now?"

I considered. "I think maybe sleeping on it might be a good idea. Unless the answer is a quick *no,* in which case it's fine to say now."

He bit his lower lip. "I like the idea of thinking about it some more. Would you move in here? Would we move into your place?"

"We would have discussions. Negotiations. We'd work something out that we both agree with. Does that make sense?"

He nodded.

"Now…how about some play?"

His eyes lit.

"Why don't we head upstairs? You've got a mat, right? For play?" Because knees on hard floors didn't always work best.

He nodded.

"Okay, why don't you get into puppy mode, and I'll be up to join you in a few minutes."

"Oh, yay." He clapped his hands. He dropped a kiss to my cheek and practically scampered up the stairs.

You've done the right thing. He needs time to think. You're always a man of action, and sometimes you railroad people into agreeing to do things when they're not ready. Waiting is good. It might've been difficult for me to conceive, but I believed my inner voice.

"Ready, Daddy."

I grinned as I headed upstairs. I'd worn jeans and a T-shirt, hoping we might play tonight.

When I entered the bedroom, I found Foster on the floor, sitting up. He'd donned puppy pajamas, his fake ears, and had a grin a mile wide. Before him lay a couple of stuffies and a rope.

Lightning quick, I grabbed the rope.

He lunged for it and managed to snag an end.

We played tug-of-war. We wrestled. We cuddled with stuffies, and he told me their stories. Most he'd found at charity stores. He'd wanted to give them second lives, and he liked the idea his money was going to do some good.

I had priced out some new stuffies. The pet store had a line of inexpensive ones, and I snagged one each of this year's variety. The money from the sales went to their pet-rescue program. I wasn't convinced they could withstand a determined dog's grip with its teeth, but I was certain Foster would take care of them. I had the lovingly wrapped gifts hidden in my SUV along with a dozen other presents. I'd gone overboard. I was all about spoiling my pup.

When he was exhausted, I asked, "Now, is Sparky ready for bed, or does Foster want something?"

"Sparky wants cuddles and then his bed...if that's okay."

"Of course it is." Foster chose his dog bed about half the time—usually after his sessions with Justin. I doubted he'd made the connection. And I wasn't going to do it for him.

I coaxed him into bed with his favorite stuffie, then I pulled the cover over him and gave him lots of scritches and kisses. He drifted off quickly. Likely tired from all the play. We'd have to do that more often, as he'd clearly enjoyed himself.

And so had I.

My own sleep was slower in coming as I worried about what Foster's answer to my question might be and whether my family would scare him away forever.

Chapter Twenty

Foster

Being warned about a family of literally thirty people versus actually sitting right in the middle of the hurricane were two very different things.

Apparently the sisters with children had gathered around noon, and the kids had opened presents and gorged on sugary treats.

Did that explain the pile of hyper kids playing with toys, fighting, speaking loudly, and laughing?

I couldn't say.

Samara, Arnav's eldest sister, handed me a hot chocolate.

I smiled gratefully.

She sat beside me so we could watch Arnav sitting with his youngest niece—whose name I embarrassingly couldn't remember—as he put together a Lego set. The intricacy of the work sort of blew my mind. I'd never had toys like that.

"You're a builder?" Samara pushed her black hair off her face.

Close up, I noted a few strands of silver.

She was my age.

I tried not to feel judged. "Uh, yes. Mostly below-market housing for families."

"That's great. My husband, Pavan—" She pointed to a man across the room who was snapping pictures of everyone.

He'd gotten me in a few, I was quite certain.

"He's a teacher. He knows so many kids who have unstable housing. Or even worse, none at all."

A pang echoed in my chest. I'd never been homeless—but we'd been close a few times. "Teaching is truly a noble profession."

She laughed. "Or a crazy one. We have four kids of our own. The eldest just started university this fall. My second one starts next year." She pointed to a young man with very floppy black hair. "Four is crazy. Or so I thought. Then Minal went and had six."

Minal, the sister closest in age to Arnav. She'd started early and been, uh, dedicated to growing her family. Six boys.

My mind whirled.

Arnav had created a family tree on posterboard for me with photos of each member of the family. Great in theory, but some of the kids kind of looked the same. Made sense since they were all cousins.

I gazed across the room and caught sight of Rashmi. I recognized the look of longing in her expression just before she caught my gaze. She raised her bottle of beer in salute to me. I wasn't certain why. And I didn't know if she was looking longingly at the kids and wishing she had some of her own, or...

For me, the longing was for family. This was what I'd missed growing up. I was so damn envious of every person here. To know this kind of unconditional love. To know someone always—always—had their backs. That was powerful stuff.

Yet I felt no longing to have a child of my own. As much as I wanted to consider fostering, that wasn't my path either. I could encourage and teach, but I couldn't care for damaged souls. Whether because I was still dealing with my own trauma, or just because I wasn't built that way, I wasn't certain. My legacy—and the continuation of PJ's hard work—was in the homes I built.

"Overwhelmed?" Samara pointed to my hot chocolate. "Drink up. Dinner's not for a few hours yet."

Heavenly smells wafted from the kitchen. Apparently Beena and Meenakshi were on dinner duty today, with Minal's husband carving the turkey. I'd been surprised at that. Apparently the family blended North American and Indian traditions seamlessly.

Arnav confided that only three of the grandchildren spoke Hindi. All were offered the choice, and only Samara's daughter and Pooja's two boys had chosen to take formal studies. The rest of the kids were exposed to the language, for certain, but without the benefits of lessons, would likely never be fluent. My *boyfriend* spoke Hindi fluently. Something he'd neglected to mention.

Pooja had dropped that little nugget to me when she'd discussed her sons' desires to one day go to India and immerse themselves in the culture and language.

As for Arnav, he sometimes took clients who spoke Hindi and was able to help guide them through the legal system.

Little things I was learning about him that made me love him more.

I sipped my hot chocolate.

Afternoon slipped into early evening, and although the samosas had been delicious, my belly wanted true sustenance. The smells emanating from the kitchen were so enticing. Reminiscent of the meals PJ had cooked for us. He'd taught me to make a whole variety of things, but the recipe cards he'd given me had been lost in one of my moves with my mother. That had devastated me more than the loss of the hockey cards I'd collected. In my mother's house, we never had the ingredients necessary to make fancy stuff. We ate basics and survived. For Howard, I'd learned to cook all his favorites. And most had been things I hadn't enjoyed, despite having what I considered an open mind.

Or maybe I hadn't liked them because he had. The one defiance I'd allowed myself.

"Dinner." Papi stood near the Christmas tree. "Mama has put everyone's name at their place. No switching them around." He pointed at one of Beena's twin daughters.

Aliyah? Man, I was trying.

Everyone rose and scrambled to the dining room.

Arnav let me know his parents had bought the house about ten years ago when his sisters just kept having kids. The dining room ran along an entire length of the house, and all thirty family members could fit. And wasn't I lucky that Samara's oldest son hadn't come home from university in Toronto so a seat was vacant for me?

I didn't dare ask what would happen if a sister decided to have another child. As I gazed over the chaos—and the longest table I'd ever seen outside of a banquet hall—I was beset by nerves.

"You're here!" One of Minal's six boys pointed to a seat right smack in the middle.

"Oh, okay." I moved that way and, sure enough, my name was in lovely script tucked in next to a Christmas cracker. Okay, so they were going to open thirty of those? That would certainly make a lot of noise.

I slid into my chair, relieved to see Arnav was on one side, Samara next to me, and Rashmi directly across from me. The rest of the family appeared to have the kids clustered around their respective parents. Three chairs were replaced by highchairs, and those children were being secured even as Arnav's father shooed, pointed, and generally tried to wrangle all his grandchildren into their seats. More than one fight erupted when siblings discovered they were expected to sit next to each other.

Across from me, Rashmi winked. "You should see us during Diwali. This is nothing compared to that."

Ah. The Celebration of Lights. I'd read up on that. It sounded amazing. The festival had been the day after Arnav and I had our fateful encounter at what I thought of as Quinton's Epic Halloween Party.

We'd received our invitation to his Out-of-This-World New Year's Eve Extravaganza. We'd also agreed that attendance was pretty much mandatory. While Arnav had worked his long hours, I'd put together our outfits. Not overly elaborate...but super adorable. Very...us.

"Now, children, hush." Mama's voice rang though the huge room.

To my amazement, everyone quieted.

Mama and Papi had both, individually, asked me to refer to them as such. Mr. and Mrs. Mehta was so formal, they'd said—cajoling me into using the more familiar terms. Hell, I hadn't even called my mother anything other than *mother*. In mere hours, I'd been welcomed into this household like a long-lost relative.

"We are always grateful to be here together." Mama gazed over the assembled crew.

Arnav, who'd slipped in beside me just before his mother had commanded silence, snagged my hand under the table and squeezed.

"Especially our new family member."

Papi, who was at the other end of the table gestured to me with his head.

"Hear, hear." Minal raised her glass. "To my younger brother finally bringing home someone worthy."

Arnav bristled. "I've never brought anyone home before." He gazed at me.

The weight of those words struck me—as he'd likely intended.

"I'm hungry." Pooja's daughter announced her desire for food just as Minal's youngest banged her spoon on the tray of her highchair.

Everyone laughed.

Mama met my gaze. "You are welcome here." She pointed to the food. "Eat."

After a fraction of a pause, everyone reached for a bowl, a plate, or a serving spoon.

Arnav explained each dish as they were passed around. I was so excited that I took a little bit of everything. The Indian cuisine smelled divine and mixed with the traditional turkey, mashed potatoes, sweet potatoes, gravy, cranberry sauce, and green beans.

The noise in the dining room overwhelmed at times—so much laughter. So much happiness. So reminiscent of my time at PJ's.

I blinked several times as I ate the last of the mashed potatoes—always a favorite and the thing I always ate last. So I could savor it. Might've been a little cold by then, but I didn't care.

The task of removing plates fell to some of the older grandchildren while Papi supervised the arrival of dessert.

I groaned inwardly as I hadn't left an ounce of space. Nope. I'd filled every nook and cranny of my stomach.

"Just have a bite." Arnav whispered in my ear. "It's all good."

How does he know? Yet he always did. Sensed things sometimes before I could even express them. And maybe that should've unnerved me. But it didn't. It reassured.

I loved that he knew me so well.

Then he rose.

All conversation died as everyone turned to look at him.

My stomach clenched.

"I'm here today, with everyone I love most in the world." He rested his hand on my shoulder.

Nope. This was not going to end well. My stomach roiled. So much for him knowing me.

"We know that, Uncle Arnav. You said this last year." One of Pooja's kids held up his glass. "Now we toast, then we get goodies."

Okay...so maybe he just did this every year and—

"But this year is extra special."

Aliyah sighed.

I'd managed to figure out which of the twins she was.

"Hey." Arnav smiled. "I invited a guest here tonight because I'm hoping you'll make him feel like family."

"We already have." Samara grasped my hand. "We like him. You can keep him."

"Yes." Papi eyed me. "Say it, dear boy."

"Okay." He drew in a deep breath. "I love Foster. With all my heart."

Oh God. Oh God. Oh God. He's going to—

"He's agreed to move in with me."

My mind stuttered. Okay, just sharing what I'd agreed to this morning. His family would've found out anyway since undoubtedly they would all, at some point, come to visit. I'd worried he might have been leading up to something else.

"Into the basement?" Beena fanned herself. "Talk about moving down in the world."

If her teasing hadn't been clear, I might've been offended on Arnav's behalf. He'd yet to show me his basement suite. If the thing was half as well appointed as this home, then the thing was way nicer than my place. Size didn't always matter—quality did. My place was better than when I'd arrived, but her age was showing—despite my best efforts.

Arnav cleared his throat. "It's a long story."

"Please spare us." Mama pointed to the food. "It needs to be eaten."

"Oh, I want to hear this." Minal patted her stomach. "I don't mind letting dinner settle first."

"Speak for yourself." Pooja's husband offered Minal a pointed look. Which she pointedly ignored.

"You know I've been saving for a down payment."

Samara gently rubbed shoulders with me. Whether to assure me Arnav would get to the point, or simply to empathize with my queasiness, I wasn't certain.

"Right. Well, I have enough. Between Christmas and New Year's, I hope to buy a house, and Foster has agreed to join me." He gazed down at me. His mouth quirked. "Should I be on one knee?"

"Oh no, this is fine." I managed to squeak that out.

"Christmas and New Year's." Rashmi stifled a yawn. "That's, like, the worst time to buy."

"No, it's the worst time to sell." Arnav puffed his chest a little. "I'm hoping to find someone who's desperate."

I blinked.

"Oh, or not." He winced. "I was just thinking in terms of a deal, and—"

"I'm glad you asked him ahead of time." Papi pointed. "Would be just like you to propose this in front of the entire family. Hey, you wait your turn." He pointed to Meenakshi's daughter who was trying to steal a sweet.

I cleared my throat.

All eyes turned to me.

"I have said yes." I gazed up at Arnav. "The answer will always be *yes.*" Also because Justin and I had spoken about what might happen if Arnav suggested we move our relationship to the next level. Or if I found the courage to. I'd expressed all kinds of reservations because of how badly I'd misjudged Howard. As Justin and I worked backward, though, I realized the signs had always been there—I'd just been too naïve to see them. And Howard had known that—had exploited that.

When Justin and I spoke of my relationship with Arnav, things were the opposite. I knew where I stood. We communicated. We understood each other. And not just about the fact I wanted to be a pup some of the time. Or that I wanted a Daddy. In all other things, he treated me as an equal.

I rose, and snagged his hand, bringing it to my lips.

Mama sighed.

One of Minal's boys snickered. Which earned him a *hush now* from his mother.

"I get it." I offered a tentative smile.

Arnav blinked.

I gestured around the table. "You share everything with your family."

"Not everything," he murmured.

"Well, I should hope not." Samara snickered.

Arnav glanced around me to give his sister the side-eye. Then he straightened and gazed down at me. "I didn't think this through. Just...you remember that case? Well I billed a lot of hours. I did a bunch for free as well. My client's uncle paid the bill in full. Even after my expenses, I did well."

"Don't forget you have to pay tax on that." Rashmi wagged her finger at him.

"Oh yes, my darling accountant sister. You will have fun doing my taxes this year."

"Move in together and live in sin for a year, and you become common-law spouses." She pointed to the sweets. "Seriously?" She pouted at her mother.

"Spouses?" My heart seized. Not in panic, but in joy. I really could see us together forever. Which was nuts. Right?

"We'd prefer you marry before moving in together, but we're traditionalists." Papi eyed me. "Don't feel bulldozed into doing something you're not ready for."

"I'm not." I managed to stammer that.

"Good. Now everyone, eat."

Despite everyone having consumed a huge dinner mere moments ago, they all descended like locusts on the desserts.

Arnav pressed a kiss to my cheek. "If we don't join in, there won't be anything left."

"I'll keep some safe for you." Samara nodded at the two of us. "Go talk it out." She snagged a plate and piled it high with desserts.

"Right." He grabbed my hand and led me out of the warm dining room. "Grab your coat. Let's go outside."

"Well, that's a way to cool down."

He arched an eyebrow. "I'll always know how to warm you up."

And so we grabbed our coats, shoved our feet into our shoes, and headed outside.

Chapter Twenty-One

Arnav

As we stepped onto the back porch, the cold air hit me in the face. *We're not staying out here long.* I leaned against the railing that had been cleared of the snow that had fallen last night.

The moon shone brightly, competing with the illumination from the streetlight down the street. My parents had a large property, but I could spot lights on in their neighbors' houses.

Foster didn't huddle like I did. He wore a warm jacket and had the air of a man who regularly worked outside in the cold.

"Are you okay?" I tried to discern his features in the darkness. *Maybe this wasn't such a great place to talk.* No doubt I was in shadow as well.

He cocked his head. "I'm okay. Why would you think I wasn't okay?" He offered a smile.

I couldn't tell if that smile was tight or genuine.

"Because I just, as my father said, bulldozed you. I didn't mean to. Just, in the middle of all that…"

"Love?"

"Yeah." *He gets it.* "They mean everything to me. You mean everything to me. It all sort of came together. I should've waited. Until you said it was okay. And then to do it in private, but…" For a lawyer, the words weren't coming easily. Things could have gone so badly wrong. Hell, they still might.

He grasped my hands. "We really should be wearing gloves."

I made a noise of agreement in my throat.

"So we won't stay out here long. Just long enough for me to assure you that you didn't do anything wrong. We've talked about the big stuff, Arnav. The really big stuff."

"Having kids. Moving in. The pup and Daddy stuff."

He nodded. "From the first moment I saw you at Club Kink, I knew you were someone who would understand. That you were putting yourself out there as much as I was."

"Plus Quinton's party."

A laugh escaped him. "Yes, well, that is a memory I'll cherish. How we met was unorthodox. My feelings for you aren't. Even if I never sleep in my dog bed again, I'll still be happy. I just want you."

I pressed my finger to his lips. "I want you to be happy, and I know, for you, that means being a pup. I'm hoping one day we can return to Kink. That you'll be comfortable playing with the other pups. That I can hang out with the Daddies and trade stories of our scamps." I fingered the leather in my pocket. "I have a gift for you. Obviously something we're not going to tell my family about."

He grinned, his white teeth shining. "Oh, something tells me that I'm going to enjoy this." He ducked his head. "Daddy."

"Oh, you know me well." I removed the gift. "I should've wrapped it or put it in a box or something. I bought it on the way home from work yesterday, and maybe I should've given it to you this morning—"

"You gave me presents this morning."

That was true. But they felt small in comparison to what he meant to me.

He leaned over to whisper in my ear. "All the toys and the blow job. Remember that?"

My cock sat up and took notice. "Uh, yeah, that. Well, plenty more where those come from." I pressed my gift into his hands.

For a moment, he stood stock still. Slowly, he fingered the studded leather. "Is this...?"

"Yep. In turquoise, because I know that's your favorite color. It suits you. But we can always return it. There are fancier ones. Ones with patterns. You know, I almost bought a plaid one. In fact, I think I might go back—"

He cut me off with a massive bear hug.

"Oof." The breath was nearly stolen from me. But I didn't care. Nothing else mattered except his evident happiness.

He rubbed his cheek against mine.

Scenting me.

He did that frequently. As if he couldn't get close enough to me.

I didn't mind in the least.

Finally, he pulled back, but grasped my hands.

I squeezed them. "Look, I plan to get something more elaborate for when we go out. This is for us."

"I'm sort of crying." He sniffed.

"From happiness, I hope."

"Yeah."

"Okay." I guided his hand to tuck the collar into his pocket and then coaxed him to zip it up. "You know..."

"Know?" He sniffed again.

"I know a couple who got married today. Adam and Dean. Up at Healing Horses Ranch."

"Okay, I heard something about that."

"Maybe one day we could, you know..."

"Get married?" He laughed. "First you ask me to live in sin with you, and *then* you suggest we might marry?"

"Backwards?"

"For us? No." He caressed my cheek—much as I often did for him. "I know this is nuts. Truly."

"Time doesn't make a relationship more solid."

He stilled.

"I'm sorry—"

"No." He pushed the word out. "I never felt for him the way I feel for you. And not just because you understand me—although that's a big part of it. But because you've never judged. The attraction I felt for you was well, explosive. Hence the blow job in an upstairs bedroom with thirty people below at the party."

I cleared my throat. My toes were going numb.

"I can see my life with you. Us both working. Us both doing volunteer stuff that fills our souls. Coming home together each night to cuddle and make love. Time with our friends. Time with your family—"

"My nutty family—"

"Your loving family." He smiled—hard to see in the shadows, but there nonetheless. "We're going to make it through. I see forever." He swallowed audibly. "And I hate that I'm going to go first and leave you alone—"

I pressed my finger to his lips. "We've got a hell of a long way to go before that's something we need to worry about." I wanted to point out that my cousin had died from cancer last year. And she'd been Samara's age. Time wasn't guaranteed. We needed to grab what we'd been given and live every moment to the fullest.

Those words didn't come. Instead, I removed my finger and replaced it with my lips.

He grasped the back of my neck and pulled me in for a drugging kiss. He made me feel like we were going to be that way forever.

The sound of the sliding glass door had us pulling apart.

"Papi says come inside or your balls will freeze off." Rashmi laughed.

"He did *not* say that." I linked arms with Foster and tugged him toward the door. My balls weren't frozen—yet—but they were trying to climb back inside my body.

"I think I'm blushing." Foster directed the comment to Rashmi.

She linked arms with him even as we toed off our shoes—which we hadn't done up or anything. "I think you're going to get along just fine in this family."

I nearly made a snide comment about her divorce, but I caught myself. A couple of times today, I'd seen her looking sad. Whether because of the children she might've wanted but didn't have, or because of the loving relationships her siblings were in—which she no longer had—I couldn't be certain. Regardless, teasing her didn't feel right.

Foster pecked her cheek. "I think I'm going to be okay too."

And so we were.

Epilogue

Foster

As we stepped up to Quinton's door, a strange feeling seized me.

"Hey, are you okay?" Arnav turned me to face him. "You said you were fine with coming back here. Were you lying to me?" He peered down at me. His expression of concern was clear, even in the porch light.

"I'm fine." *Nervous. But fine.*

He didn't look convinced.

I pressed a kiss to his lips

Just as the door opened.

"Oh, I thought I saw someone coming up the walkway." Quinton opened the door wider. "You've got to get in here. Things are just getting interesting."

As always, I had no idea what he was talking about. Still, I snagged Arnav's hand and led him into the house.

A blast of warm air hit me, and I reveled in it.

The winds had picked up, and again the threat of snow lingered. Just a light flurry, though. In the early morning.

As much as I loved Quinton, I wasn't going to get stuck here in a snowstorm. My pickup truck was parked on the street, and we were out of there at the first sign of real snow.

Quinton hugged me tightly. "So glad you made it."

"Yeah, me too." I held on for just a bit longer. This was the man who'd seen my loneliness and had sort of dragged me into his circle. Thanks to him, I'd met the love of my life.

"Hey, what about me?" Arnav laughed. "Don't I get love?"

After releasing me, Quinton grabbed him. "Of course you do. Sometimes people need extra love." He finished the hug, then turned back to me. "All is well?"

"Yeah." I'd considered telling Quinton about my kink. He'd have understood—I was certain of that. Still, I hesitated. Arnav and I had a date for the last Wednesday in January. Pup night at Club Kink. I'd already been in touch with Evan to get his advice, and he promised to come along to introduce me to all the pups.

Arnav planned to watch over me, but to also socialize with some of the other handlers. See if he could pick up any tricks. He was learning.

So was I.

"If it isn't the hotshot lawyer." A tall, dark, and imposing man headed our way. He was even taller than Arnav. He held out his hand. "Counselor."

Arnav ginned. "Counselor." He shook the man's hand. "Nice to see you, Zach."

I toed off my shoes.

"You did good work." Zach grinned. "Bested one of my finest prosecutors."

Arnav stood a little taller. "I did my job."

"And then some. You found what our forensic accountants didn't."

"That's true." He scratched his clean-shaven jaw. "But I believed my client was innocent and so went in with that mindset. Your prosecutor looked at the evidence and, on the surface, it made my client look guilty. Just two different perspectives on the same set of facts."

Zach raised an eyebrow. His dark hair and eyes gave him a roguish look I found both sexy and intimidating. "Still, well done."

"Thank you." Arnav pulled his arm around my waist. "I don't think you've met Foster." He pressed a kiss to my temple, then turned back to Zach. "The love of my life."

"Really?" Zach grinned. "I love when people find their soulmates." For just a moment, his happiness slipped.

Just a fraction of a second, but the pain in his eyes hit me. Pain I'd seen many times in the mirror when I'd been with Howard—the pain of missing something in life. So was Zach just lonely or was he pining for someone from his past? I was truly curious.

And none of your damn business.

Zach shook my hand. "Lovely to meet you, Foster. Why don't you guys take your coats off? I can get you drinks, and Arnav can regale us with his exploits. Everett's already here."

He pointed to a striking Black man who was huddled with two men I recognized from the Halloween party. A tall ginger with blue eyes and an adorable beard as well as an Indian man.

Arnav laughed. "Everett's holding court with Ravi and Maddox? Why am I not surprised?"

"I think Justin and Stanley are in the kitchen." Zach looked around. "Adam and Dean are on their honeymoon. Ravi filled me in—sleigh rides on Christmas Day."

"Sounds like a nice wedding." I remembered Arnav saying the men had married at Healing Horses. I could imagine sleigh rides on the ranch.

"Who are they?" Arnav leaned a little closer to Zach while indicating a couple I hadn't noticed. The taller one was blond, hunky, and gorgeous. His hazel eyes shone in the light. Next to him was a ginger with a trimmed beard and blue eyes.

"Oh, that's Simeon and Ryan." Zach grinned. "Quinton met them at Maddox's infamous Christmas cocktail party."

Arnav snickered. "I don't generally associate Maddox and infamous. Seeing as he's the father of twin toddlers, I see him as more sedate."

"Well, you'll laugh. Ryan told us the story about that night. The night of the massive snowstorm? His car was buried, and he had to go home with Simeon. And they rescued a dog from the road and..." Zach squinted. "I think they're moving in together."

"*The* snowstorm?" I snagged Arnav's arm and with more bravery than sense, said, "We might've enjoyed being snowed in that night as well."

"Really?" Zach grinned. "Come join the group and you can swap stories. Only wait for me. What would you like to drink?"

"Hot chocolate." Arnav searched my face.

I nodded.

"Two hot chocolates coming up." Zach nodded and headed toward the kitchen.

"Maybe we should take off our coats?" Arnav laughed. "Seeing as we've already been here for about ten minutes."

"I am getting warm." I removed my coat and handed it to my boyfriend who hung them both in the closet. "Zach really wanted to greet you."

"You remember I told you I spoke to Remy Stevens?"

I searched my memory. "Right. You told me Christmas Eve, and her husband's name is Rusty." Heat crept into my cheeks.

Arnav kissed my nose. "I prefer Sparky."

"So do I." And my collar sat at the front door at home. Arnav had pretty much moved into my place. We'd found our dream home just the day before, with the help of our trusted realtor, Cadence. A lovely three-bedroom house with a large backyard and a massive dining room. Wouldn't fit thirty, but we'd come close. The basement also had a gigantic rec room. Great for romping around in. Whether me as a pup or for some of Arnav's many, many, many nieces and nephews.

I'd given notice to my landlord just in time—his daughter wanted to move in with her boyfriend. Frank wasn't thrilled about her decision, but believed it better to have the couple close by. So he was giving discounted rent to the two as they got their start in life. I was incredibly glad I'd done the renovations. His daughter was a genuine and respectful young woman. Knowing she'd have a nice place to live made me glow inside.

"Two hot chocolates." Zach eyed us. "You haven't moved."

"Hey, we were having a moment." Arnav took a mug, then handed it to me.

Zach handed him the second one. "I still want you to meet Ryan and Simeon."

"Because you want to hear our snowstorm story." I arched an eyebrow at him, feeling confident in a way I hadn't in a long time.

Possibly ever.

"Guilty as charged." Zach led us over to the group of gathered men. The next hour passed quickly as we discussed snowstorms and one-bed scenarios. Turned out Maddox and Ravi had a snowstorm story of their own which had Ravi laughing and Maddox blushing.

Simeon didn't speak as much as Ryan—possibly because of his stutter or possibly just because of his reserved nature. The two made an adorable couple.

I caught Everett looking around for the dozenth time. As Zach was recounting something to do with a courtroom, I'd have thought the lawyer next to me would be interested, but he was scanning the crowd again. "Are you looking for someone?"

He pursed his lips. "That obvious?"

"Well..." I eyed him. "I pay attention—when I can. You intrigue me."

He arched an eyebrow.

Heat crept into my cheeks. "Well, I don't know many gay men in Mission City, let alone other Black ones."

"Ah. Well, I hope you're welcomed everywhere. If not, let me know." He snickered. "There's another lawyer, Gil. And the harbormaster Isaac. Oh, and an arborist." He gazed upward. "August." He met my gaze again. "And plenty of other folk whom I can't name at the moment. The gay local community is also welcoming. Again, that I've found."

Arnav gently grasped my hand, even as he continued to engage Zach in some discussion about a case they faced off on last year.

I blinked at Everett. "Yeah. I think I've found my people."

He grinned. "And your person."

"Uh, yeah." I squeezed Arnav's hand and I received a squeeze in return.

I refocused on Everett. "So who's this guy you're looking for? He's not here, I take it?"

He shook his head. "We, uh..." He winced.

I grinned. "Look, Arnav and I have a story in this house as well. Something about an upstairs bedroom?" I couldn't believe I was being so bold. But something about Everett's hangdog look had me empathizing.

"Okay." He leaned closer. "I did something really wild with a guy on Halloween, and after I cleaned up, he'd vanished. Like entirely. And no one knew who he was."

"Not even Quinton?"

"Not even." He sighed. "The guy said his name was *Rayne*, but I don't even know whether or not to believe him. And now I have no idea, and I guess I really hoped he'd be here tonight."

"So you might get a repeat?"

His dark-brown eyes met mine. "So I could talk to him."

"Oh."

"Well, and I wouldn't say *no* to more."

That had me smiling. "That's fair."

Quinton appeared with Rainbow and Justin in tow, carrying trays of champagne flutes. "Justin has the non-alcoholic, and hurry up, because midnight's coming soon."

En masse, we descended upon those brave enough to carry the trays.

Justin met my gaze and grinned as I took a flute. We had one more session planned in January, then we'd agreed he'd discharge me. I'd keep his number handy, but I honestly felt I'd worked through many of my issues. Having Arnav beside me meant everything. The acceptance. The love. I no longer grieved the losses in my life—my mother, Howard, and most importantly PJ. He'd always be a big part of my heart. He made me the man I was today. Someone I was damn proud of. Someone worthy of Arnav's love. Of his family's clear affection. Tomorrow we were all headed to Beena's house for samosas, mimosas, and general merriment.

I couldn't wait.

"All right. Counting down from ten." Quinton started us all out and we obediently followed his lead.

After the obligatory *Happy New Year*, Arnav took me in his arms. "I love you."

"Yes. That. And more."

He pressed his lips to mine. He might've coaxed my lips open.

I might've let him.

He pressed against me.

I grinned. "Anxious to go home."

Against my ear, he whispered, "Sparky, you have no idea."

My breath hitched. Oh, we were going to have fun tonight. I liked when frisky Daddy came out to play.

As the noise died down, I handed my flute to a surprised Everett and then I leapt on to the raised fireplace step. Only about a foot, but enough to put me over everyone's head. "I need everyone's attention."

To my shock, the noise died immediately.

I sought Quinton's gaze.

He saluted me with his glass.

Okay, so my plan was on. I took in a deep breath. "I don't know everyone here."

"Well, we want to know you." A gorgeous woman in the corner saluted me.

"As friends? You're on." Boldness overtook me. "I want to get to know everyone. I'm finished hiding in the corner."

A general cheer went up.

I gazed down at Arnav who gaped. "Join me."

He handed his flute to an amused Stanley, then hopped up on the brick. He leaned over. "What are you doing?" No concern or embarrassment. Only amusement.

I met his gaze. "Asking you to marry me."

"You have to say it loud enough for everyone to hear." Quinton held his hand to his ear.

I took a deep breath. Still grasping my love's hand, I turned to the crowd. "I met this amazing man during the Halloween party here."

Quinton raised his hand. "He's talking about me."

The crowd hooted.

I held up my hand—locked with Arnav. "But I got scared."

A general *aw* went up through the crowd.

"But we met again." *Don't blush.* "And we realized..." I gazed into his eyes. "We're meant to be together."

"Woo-hoo!" Ravi clapped

Maddox rolled his eyes at his husband.

I grinned. "So this guy asks me to move in with him the very first time I meet his massive family." I gazed around the room. "Massive." I pressed a kiss to Arnav's knuckles. "And I was totally intimidated."

"I'd say so." Stanley chuckled as he pointed to Justin. "You should've seen me with this guy's family."

Justin beamed.

"But they welcomed me." I gazed across the room. "Just like you all have. I mean, I haven't met all of you—"

"We'll rectify that." Another woman raised her glass. "You keep right on going—we've got your back."

I nodded. "So, I don't want to live in sin."

Quinton hooted.

Several people laughed.

"Which means getting married by the end of the month."

Rainbow raised her hand. "I know a possible wedding venue. Apparently, my ranch is the latest *it* destination."

I offered my glass in salute. "My future mother-in-law has this all in hand." I glanced at Arnav. "If you say *yes*."

"Mama?" He whispered the word reverentially.

"Yes." I leaned closer. "I asked your parents. If they weren't okay with it—"

"I wouldn't have cared." He spat the words out fiercely.

"But I would have." I grinned. "Rashmi softened the way. We're good...if you say *yes*."

"Way to make us wait." Everett nudged Arnav. "If you hadn't spent the entire night gazing at your man in awe, I might not be encouraging you so vehemently. After all, you've only known each other two months."

Arnav blinked. "Some people can know in five minutes, and some will spend a lifetime searching. I've found the man I want to spend the rest of my life with."

"So that's a *yes*?" Quinton rolled his hand yet again, clearly wanting us to move this along.

My love gazed into my eyes. "It's a *yes*."

The room erupted into the loudest cheer I'd ever heard. I worried the neighbors might call the cops, then remembered plenty of people were igniting firecrackers. Tonight was for celebration. For new beginnings. For cementing love.

This time, I pulled him into my arms. "I love you." I leaned in close. "Daddy."

He matched my grin. "Yes, Sparky." He could use that name with me, and people would think the name was a term of endearment.

I cocked my head. "What are we going to name our actual dog?"

He blinked.

"The one we're going to rescue once we're married and settled in the house? Because that backyard is just begging for a pooch."

"You can always borrow Princess Sofia." Maddox leaned over. "Sorry, had to listen in. I didn't do the public proposal, and I'm finding this fascinating."

"I take it Princess Sofia is a dog?" I leaned toward the ginger lumberjack.

"Well, yes, she is." Maddox scratched his beard. "She's...unique."

"Great. We can borrow her to test out what it'll be like." I nearly vibrated with excitement. "This is perfect."

"You're perfect." Arnav kissed my cheek.

"Okay, photo time!" Quinton moved toward us with a fancy-assed camera. Apparently he'd taken my request to make tonight special to heart. "Everyone make way."

The red seas parted. Well, the partygoers.

"One of them together alone, and then one with all of us. To commemorate the fabulousness." Quinton ran his hand up and down his pink sequined jacket.

The one I'd somehow not noticed before now.

Or had he just put it on?

I was too befuddled to figure it out.

We took pictures. Lots and lots and lots of pictures.

And that night, cuddled against my daddy and wearing my collar, I dreamed of big houses, large yards, and lots of rescue dogs.

Want to know about Everett's mystery man?

Check the next book in the *Love in Mission City* series, set in beautiful British Columbia.

Rayne's Return (Love in Mission City Book 4)

Also available:

Ginger Snapping All the Way (Love in Mission City Book 1)

Stanley's Christmas Redemption (Love in Mission City Book 2)

Sleigh Bells and Second Chances (Love in Mission City Book 3)

The Beauty of the Beast(Love in Mission City Book 3.5)

Rayne's Return (Love in Mission City Book 4)

Love in Mission City: The Boyfriends Duet

Love in Mission City: The Shorts

Page Against the Machine

The Lightkeeper's Love Affair

Ace's Place

Marcus's Cadence

Not in it for the Money

Also:

Axe to Grind

Grindstone's Edge

Hugh (Single Dads of Gaynor Beach)

Anthony (Single Dads of Gaynor Beach)

Xavier (Single Dads of Gaynor Beach)

Love Furever (Friends of Gaynor Beach Animal Rescue)

Husky Love (Friends of Gaynor Beach Animal Rescue)

My Past, Your Future

If Only for Today

Catch a Tiger by the Tail

Solstice Surprise

Valentino in Vancouver

You See Me

Sun, Surf, and Surprises

Love Without Reservations

An Uncommon Gentleman

Caressa's Homecoming (Bound by Love Book 1)

Cole's Reckoning (Bound by Love Book 2)

Didn't See You Coming

Audiobooks

Ginger Snapping All the Way

Stanley's Christmas Redemption

Sleigh Bells and Second Chances

Love in Mission City: The Shorts

Page Against the Machine

The Lightkeeper's Love Affair

Ace's Place

Marcus's Cadence

Not in it for the Money

Hugh (Single Dads of Gaynor Beach)

Anthony (Single Dads of Gaynor Beach)

Love Furever (Friends of Gaynor Beach Animal Rescue)

My Past, Your Future

If Only for Today

Catch a Tiger by the Tail

Solstice Surprise

An Uncommon Gentleman

Didn't See You Coming – coming soon

Want a free short story? The story is set in Gaynor Beach, California where there are plenty of single dads and puppy rescues! You can sign up for my newsletter so you can keep up with all the great stuff I'm doing as well as pictures of my own pooches, Ally and Finnegan.

Hemingway's Happy Day

Love contemporary MF romances? What's better than love in the beautiful Cedar Valley in British Columbia, Canada? Find small town romances with a touch of angst, a bit of heat, and a lot of heart...

The Absolution of Abigail Reardon (prequel)
The Luminosity of Loriana Harper (Book 1)
The Making of Marnie Jones (Book 2)
The Redemption of Remy St. Claire (Book 3)

Interested in knowing more about Gabbi?

Sign up for her newsletter
Follow her on Bookbub
Follow her on Instagram

USA Today Bestselling author Gabbi Grey lives in beautiful British Columbia where her fur baby chin-poo keeps her safe from the nasty neighborhood squirrels. Working for the government by day, she spends her early mornings writing contemporary, gay, sweet, and dark erotic BDSM romances. While she firmly believes in happy endings, she also believes in making her characters suffer before finding their true love. She also writes m/f romances as Gabbi Black and Gabbi Powell.

Manufactured by Amazon.ca
Acheson, AB